CADE MCCALL: ARMY SCOUT

THE WESTERN ADVENTURES OF CADE MCCALL
BOOK V

ROBERT VAUGHAN

WOLFPACK
PUBLISHING
— EST 2013 —

Cade McCall Army Scout

Paperback Edition
Copyright © 2019 Robert Vaughan

Wolfpack Publishing
6032 Wheat Penny Ave
Las Vegas, NV 89122

wolfpackpublishing.com

Paperback ISBN 978-1-64119-824-0
eBook ISBN 978-1-64119-825-7

CADE MCCALL: ARMY SCOUT

PROLOGUE

Twin Creek Ranch, Howard County, Texas – 1927

OWEN WISTER HAD BECOME A FREQUENT VISITOR TO TWIN CREEK Ranch as he gathered material for the in-depth biography he was writing about his friend, Cade McCall. At the moment, he and Cade were alone in the library at Cade's house.

Wister saw something he hadn't noticed before. It was a rather small shadow box that hung alone, away from the myriad of awards and memorabilia that covered the open spaces in the room. He got up from his chair and walked over to the box for a closer examination. What he saw was a star-shaped medal pinned to a felt backing, displayed in a gold frame.

"Good Lord, Cade, is this the Medal of Honor?" Wister asked.

"It is," Cade said. "Amos Chapman, Billy Dixon, and I received the medal for our role in what became known as the 'Buffalo Wallow Fight.'"

Wister reached up to touch it. "The Medal of Honor. Very impressive."

"It'd be more impressive if I could actually claim it."

1

At the strange comment, Wister looked at Cade. "What do mean, if you could claim it?"

"The government took the medal away from us back in 1916," Cade said. He laughed. "I suppose 'rescinded' would be a better way of putting it. They didn't actually send someone out here to physically reclaim the medal."

"In 1916? That had to be more than forty years after the battle. Why would they change their minds so many years later?"

"It was forty-two years, to be exact. The powers that be decided no civilian could be awarded the Medal of Honor, and since Amos, Billy and I were *civilian* scouts for the Army...well, that was the way it happened. We lost the Medal of Honor. Billy didn't know because he died in 1913, but Amos and I—we knew." Cade was quiet for a while as he looked away. "You know, Amos lost a leg in that little skirmish, but that didn't mean anything to the War Department. He died a couple of years ago."

"That doesn't seem right," Wister exclaimed. "I can see how the Army might change its mind and say civilians are no longer eligible, but I don't think that ruling should be retroactive."

Cade smiled. "That's why you're a writer and not a bureaucrat.

There was a light tap on the door.

"Yes, come in," Cade called.

A very pretty young woman stepped into the library.

"Mr. Wister, Grandpa, Grandma says supper is ready," Amanda told them.

"Thank you, darlin'. Dan, after you," Cade said, calling Owen Wister by the name his family and friends used.

Molly greeted them in the dining room.

"Did you fry the fish?" Cade asked. "If it isn't fried, I won't eat it."

"Cade McCall, we've been married for more than forty years. Why is it you've never told me before that you prefer it fried?"

"What?"

Amanda laughed. "It's fried, Grandpa. Grandma's just teasing you."

"So, are we about to get into the tale of your days as an Army scout?" Owen asked as his plate was set before him."

"That, and the German girls," Cade replied.

"German girls?' Owen asked, confused by the reference. "What do girls from Germany have to do with it?"

"That was their name, not what country they came from. The German girls."

"It's hard to think of Mrs. Feldman as a girl," Amanda said with a little laugh. "She's an old lady now."

"When I first met Sophia Feldman, she was Sophia German, and she was a young girl."

"You said German 'girls,' so I take it there were more than just the one," Owen said.

Cade nodded. "Those girls had a big influence on the course of the Red River War, and I have a feeling that's what you'll want to hear about next," Cade said. "But it's going to take a little while to get into the story, so if you don't mind, we will get started on it in the morning."

1

"ARE YOU SURE YOU WANT TO DO THIS?" JETER WILLIS ASKED AS CADE saddled a sorrel horse he had bought from the livery stable. "You can always come back and be a partner in the Red House."

"I appreciate the offer, Jeter. I really do," Cade replied. "But I'm going to see what's going on in Texas."

"Don't tell me you're going back to Adobe Walls? Or are you going to try and find Jacob Harrison?" Jeter asked. "You know, he sent word that he wants to join the Texas Rangers."

"It's neither Adobe Walls or Jacob," Cade said. "I've been thinking about going out to Fort Dodge and seeing if Billy Dixon is still around. Didn't you say he has a job scouting for the Army? I might want to join up."

"You do know who the commandant of Fort Dodge is, don't you?"

"I heard it's Nelson Miles."

"Yes," Jeter confirmed. "Some of the soldiers who come in here tell about the Battle of Chancellorsville. They say Miles was as tough as nails."

"But as I recall, the South won that battle."

"We did, but in the end, it didn't matter. They say Miles took a bullet in the belly and survived," Jeter said.

ROBERT VAUGHAN

Cade swung up onto the saddle. "Good for him."

Jeter extended his hand to Cade. "You, more than any of us, have a reason to hate the men in blue, and everyone at Fort Dodge is wearing a blue uniform."

"I know, but at the Walls, there were Yankees and Rebels, and we all fought together. It's been close to ten years since I got out of that Yankee hellhole prison, and there's been a lot of water pass under the bridge since then. If the Yankee soldiers are all right with me, I'll be all right with them."

Fort Dodge

FORT DODGE WAS SITUATED on the left bank of the Arkansas River, about five miles northwest of Dodge City. It was roughly halfway between the Cimarron Crossing and the Mulberry Creek Crossing, the points used most frequently by the Indians to ford the Arkansas River. Its original purposes were to protect the Santa Fe Trail and to serve as a base against hostile Indian operations.

Although the post wasn't surrounded by palisades, as were many Western posts, it did have a guard on the road at the entry. As Cade approached, he was challenged by the sentry.

"Dismount," the guard said.

Cade did as he was ordered.

"Are you a soldier out of uniform or a civilian?" the guard asked. He was holding his rifle at "port arms," meaning he was holding it so that it cut a forty-five-degree angle across his chest.

"I'm a civilian."

"State your name and the purpose of your visit, sir."

"I'm Cade McCall, and I'm here to see Billy Dixon. I think he is one of the civilian scouts."

A huge smile spread across the soldier's face, and he lowered his weapon. "You're Cade McCall?"

"Yes," Cade replied, a little confused that the guard seemed to recognize his name.

"You 'n Dixon. You two was the ones that ended the fight at Adobe Walls by makin' them long shots. How far away was that Injun you kilt?"

"I'm not sure."

"I heard it was over a mile!" the soldier said, clearly impressed. He stepped back and gave a welcoming wave with his hand.

"Go on in, Mr. McCall, 'n if you're a' lookin' for Billy Dixon, you'll more 'n likely find him havin' a beer at the Sutler Store, which is exactly where I'm goin' to be headin' soon as my relief shows up."

"Thank you, Private..."

"It's Bledsoe, sir."

"Thank you, Private Bledsoe."

It was easy to find because unlike all the other drab-looking, unpainted buildings on the post, the Sutler store was painted blue and trimmed in red. It also had a sign which proclaimed not only that this was the Sutler Store, but the proprietor was A.J. Anthony.

After dismounting and tying off his horse, Cade stepped inside. The store was redolent of fresh coffee and tobacco smoke. Here the soldiers could buy combs, shaving brushes, shaving cups, the cans of peaches or tomatoes which were popular items, and just about anything a civilian could buy in a store on Main Street in any town.

The Sutler Store was also a club of sorts, with separate rooms for the officers and civilians. Here the officers, soldiers, and civilian employees could buy whiskey, beer, and even soft drinks. The scouts' position was unique, in that they could associate with the officers or the enlisted men on an equal footing.

CADE HEARD a familiar voice in the middle of a story.

"So Amos says, 'Billy, me 'n you's got to outrun that bear.' 'N I said to him, 'I don't have to outrun the bear. I only got to outrun you.'"

The soldiers at the table broke into laughter.

"Still telling that bear story, I see. Well, it's as funny now as it was the first time I heard it," Cade said, smiling as he approached the table where Billy Dixon sat with another civilian and half a dozen soldiers.

"Cade McCall! You old devil," Dixon said, getting up from the table and coming toward him with his hand extended. "I knew damn well you wouldn't stay back there in Tennessee."

"From what Jeter told me about his bet, I'm about the only one who didn't know that," Cade replied.

"Fellas, you've all heard about the fifteen-hundred-'n-thirty-eight-yard-long shot I made at Adobe Walls. This is Cade McCall, and he made a long shot at the same time. Of course, his was only fifteen hundred and eighteen yards long."

"Your shot was twenty yards longer?" one of the soldiers asked.

"Indeed, it was."

"What do you say about that, Mr. McCall?"

Cade laughed. "Every time Billy tells the story, he takes off another couple of yards of mine and adds another couple to his own. By this time next year, his shot will be two miles long, and it'll probably be that I didn't shoot the Indian at all. I just reached out and tapped him on the head with a stick."

Billy laughed at Cade's response, then called for a beer to be brought over to his friend. After the beer and some visiting, Billy set his glass down, wiped his mouth, and asked the question he had been wondering about.

"What brings you out to the fort? I figured you would stay in Dodge."

"Jacob's gone to Texas, which means there's no Harrison and McCall freight line, and Jeter's got the Red House Salon, so that leaves me with nothing to do."

"'Red House Salon?' Are you talking about the saloon?" one of the soldiers asked.

"Yes, the saloon," Cade said without further amplification.

"What kind of work would you be lookin' for?" Billy asked.

"I heard you were scouting for the Army. I thought I might try something like that."

"Cade, have you seen what color uniform these men are wearing?" Billy teased. "They're all Yankee soldiers."

"You was a Reb?" one of the soldiers asked.

"I started out as a Reb, but I spent the last year of the war with the soldiers in blue," Cade said

"You mean you switched sides?" a sergeant asked, shocked by the comment.

"In a matter of speaking, I did. I was captured at Franklin and spent the last year of the war at Camp Douglass, surrounded by Yankees."

"Wait. You mean you was a prisoner?" the inquisitive soldier asked, understanding now what Cade was telling him.

"Yes."

The sergeant nodded and smiled broadly. "Well, sir, then you have my respect. I wouldn't have no respect for any son of a bitch who deserted his own side 'n switched over to the enemy, be he Reb or Union."

"So you would like to be a scout, would you?" Billy asked.

"Yes, I would, and I was sort of hoping you would put in a good word for me."

"Yessiree, I will. I'll do it right now. Come on, let me introduce you to General Miles."

"General? I thought Miles was a colonel."

"Well, actually he is a colonel, but he was a brevet general durin' the war, which means he can still be called general, 'n folks that wants to stay on his good side generally call him that."

"Then I'll call him 'General.'"

Billy chuckled. "You learn real quick, don't you? I think you might work out just fine workin' for the Army."

. . .

GENERAL MILES STROKED his mustache as Billy Dixon introduced Cade.

"Yes, Mr. McCall, both Mr. Dixon and Mr. Masterson speak highly of you, and as it so happens, I do have room for another scout if you would like to join."

"What is it exactly that you have in mind, General?" Cade asked.

Miles smiled at being referred to as "General." Unlike most senior officers in the Army, Miles was not a West Point graduate. He had entered the Army as a volunteer when the Civil War began and had worked his way up to brevetted brigadier general, not in the volunteers, but in the regular Army.

"Good that you ask, Mr. McCall. It is a wise man who ascertains the depth of the water before he leaps in.

"Soon, we will begin offensive operations against the hostile Indians who for some time now have been waging war and committing atrocities against the frontier settlements. I understand you were part of the group that defended Adobe Walls, so you are quite familiar with those conditions."

"Yes, sir, I was, and I am."

"It has reached the point, Mr. McCall, that those Indians who will not return peacefully to their reservations will be killed, and quite frankly, I don't care whether they return or not."

Cade was taken aback to hear the Indian problem put in those words, especially by a general. His thoughts went to Spotted Wolf and Gentle Horse, the mother of Stone Forehead. Through an unusual set of circumstances, Cade had become the surrogate father of the half-breed Cheyenne child, and were it not for his brother and sister-in-law back in Tennessee, Stone would be with him now.

"Do you have any personal business you must take care of before we leave?" the general asked.

"No, sir, I'm ready to leave this afternoon if you so order."

General Miles chuckled. "That's the kind of eagerness I like to hear. Hold up your right hand."

Cade raised his hand, then repeated the oath as it was administered.

"*I, Cade McCall, do solemnly swear that I will support and defend the Constitution of the United States against all enemies, foreign and domestic; that I will bear true faith and allegiance to the same; and that I will obey the orders of the President of the United States and the orders of the officers appointed over me.*"

The oath administered, Cade lowered his hand.

"All right Mr. McCall, you are now on the payroll as a scout of the U.S. Army. The full-scale military operation will begin as soon as practicable. Mr. Dixon, take this man to see Lieutenant Baldwin, with my direction that he will join his command."

LIEUTENANT FRANK BALDWIN was about Cade's age, tall, slender, and with a full sweeping mustache. He seemed personable but efficient.

"You'll be paid seventy-five dollars a month, and an extra fifty dollars anytime you act as a courier. As a courier, you'll be expected to go through hostile territory, and most often, you'll be going alone. Do you anticipate any problem with that?"

"No, sir, I don't."

"Then, as our sailor friends say, welcome aboard." Baldwin extended his hand.

Cade chuckled.

"What is it?"

"The last time I sailed, I didn't exactly get a welcome aboard," Cade said.

"You were in the Navy?"

"No, but I was a sailor of sorts."

"'Of sorts?'"

"He was shanghaied, Lieutenant," Billy said. "It's one hell of a story. You'll have to get him to tell you sometime."

"I will. Oh, by the way, I don't know if Billy told you, but Bat

Masterson is a scout. Since all three of you were at Adobe Walls, it should be a reunion."

"It'll be good to have Bat around. He does keep things lively," Cade replied, thinking of the many dollars he had lost to Bat in friendly poker games. "How many scouts will there be?"

"Counting you, I now have seventeen men, most of them buffalo hunters. I expect they will be most knowledgeable about the country where our troops will be operating," Baldwin said. "And then there are twenty Delaware Indians, who are some of the best trackers I've ever met."

"Wait until you meet the chief," Billy offered.

"What about him?" Cade asked.

"Oh, don't get me wrong, Fall Leaf is as good a tracker as any of the others, and they listen to him. It's just that he is seventy years old, and his face is as wrinkled as a washboard."

"Will he be able to keep up with us?" Cade asked.

Lieutenant Baldwin laughed. "That isn't the question, Mr. McCall. The question is, are we going to be able to keep up with him?"

2

Jacob Harrison had been in the Frontier Battalion of the Texas Rangers for well over a month when he was summoned before Major John B. Jones, the commanding officer.

"Harrison, I've been told you once owned a freight wagon company. Is that correct?"

"Yes, sir."

"Then may I take it that you're quite skilled at driving a wagon?"

"I'd say I am."

"Good, good. There's been some Indian trouble up around Jack County," Major Jones said. "I'm going to take twenty men into the field, and I'll need a wagon to carry the extra equipment we might need. What I'm asking is, considering the rough country we'll be going through and the pace I'd like to maintain, do you think you'd be able to keep up with me if I asked you to drive?"

"Major, if any man alive can keep up with you, I can do it," Jacob replied, "providing I've got good stock to pull the wagon."

Jones laughed and reached out to take Jacob's hand. "That's exactly the attitude I like, and you're just the man I want. We leave tomorrow, so you might want to go to the stable and select your team."

. . .

WITH MAJOR JONES in the lead, the twenty-man detail started toward Salt Creek, where an earlier scout had found Indian sign. Because he didn't want the Indians to get away, Jones set a ground-eating pace that made it difficult for Jacob to keep up, but he did it. They covered fifteen miles in less than two hours.

Here the terrain was much more difficult since they were in the mountains, and the road, which was little more than a narrow, rutted slag-strewn path, was barely wide enough to accommodate the wagon. They were about halfway between Belknap and Jacksboro when Major Jones called a halt. Since they were on a creek, Jacob thought the stop had been called to rest the horses, and he welcomed it.

As he soon learned, though, this wasn't just a rest break. An advance scout had spotted Indians just ahead in a place called Lost Valley. Major Jones called his men together.

"Rangers, we've made good time this morning, and it would appear we've caught up with the devils. Ranger Corn has been on scout and he tells me that when we go into the valley, we'll be ambushed by about thirty Indians.

"But here's the thing about ambushes. They really only work when they're launched by surprise, and because we know they're there, they won't be able to surprise us. And since there are only thirty of them, we'll have them outnumbered."

"Sir, did you say there were thirty Indians?" Ranger Moore asked.

"I did."

"But we only got twenty men."

"Yes, twenty *Rangers* against thirty *Indians*." Major Jones smiled. "As I said, we'll have them outnumbered."

The others, catching the emphasis on the words "Rangers" and "Indians," realized what Major Jones was saying, and they all laughed.

"To horse, Rangers. In we go."

Jacob climbed back onto the wagon seat, unwound the reins from the lever, released the brake, and waited for the order.

"At a gallop!" Major Jones called. "Forward, ho!"

Jacob snapped the reins, and that was all that was needed. The team, which had been keeping up with the horses for the entire day, broke into a gallop so as not to lose connection. Horses, men, and wagon covered the half-mile to the valley opening in less than two minutes. And as expected, their arrival was greeted by a volley of gunfire from Indians concealed behind rocks, trees, and even an earthen berm.

What was unexpected was the volume of the gunfire from the Indians, and a dozen horses went down in the opening fusillade. Finding himself with more than half his command unhorsed, Major Jones had no choice but to order the rest of his men to dismount and return fire.

Before Jacob was able to jump down from the wagon, both of his horses were hit, and with startled cries of pain, both animals went down. Jacob, who was armed only with a pistol, dashed across an open area and joined the rest of the Ranger force in a ravine that offered some cover against the fire from the Indians.

"Major, looks to me like there's more 'n any thirty Indians here," one of the Rangers said. "I mean, there's that thirty we was told about down here, 'n there's just a whole lot of 'em up there on the side of the mountain, too."

"I know," Major Jones said. "It would appear they did have an element of surprise."

"What'll we do?"

"We'll do what we have to do," Major Jones said. "We'll remain here, at least until nightfall. In the meantime, horde your ammunition, and shoot only when you have a..."

Major Jones' admonition to horde ammunition was interrupted by a gunshot, and everyone looked toward Jacob, who was holding a smoking pistol in his hand.

Jacob said nothing, but with a nod of his head, he indicated the opposite end of the depression. There, an Indian lay face down in the dirt, a war-club in one hand and a knife in the other.

Over the next several hours, the Rangers were able to hold the

Indians at bay, but Indians held the Rangers in a siege. There was no way for the Rangers to escape, but on the other hand, every time one, or even several, Indians tried to take advantage of the situation, they were shot down.

"Major, we've got to have some water," Ranger Bailey said. "All our canteens was left on our horses."

"Yeah, 'n this sun is cookin' us pretty good," Moore added.

"How are you going to do it?" Major Jones asked. "By the time you filled enough canteens to do any good, you'd be exposed for too long."

"I was thinkin' about that," Ranger Corn said. "They's two barrels of water on the ambulance. They're too heavy for one man to carry, but if four of us was to go out there, there'd be two apiece on the barrels, 'n we could get 'em back."

"That's a job for volunteers," Major Jones replied. "I have no intention of issuing such an order."

"Well, hell, Major, me 'n Moore can go," Bailey offered. Moore nodded in agreement.

"And that'll be three of us," Moore added.

Jacob started to volunteer, but before he could do so, Ranger Glass spoke up. "I'll go, too."

"All right, men. Do what you can," Major Jones said.

The four men crawled out of the ravine and, bending over at the waist, ran to the wagon. Their movement was so unexpected that not one shot was fired at them.

"Damn! They made it," Ranger Anderson said.

If the Indians had let them get to the wagon unmolested, they didn't neglect them now. At least half a dozen flaming arrows arched through the air, and within a moment, the wagon was ablaze.

"Them sons of bitches is burnin' 'em alive!" one of the Rangers shouted in outrage.

"No," Major Jones said, "here they come. Open fire, men, and give them cover!"

The four men, two to a barrel, were running back. But, burdened by the load they were carrying, they couldn't come back as fast as they had gone out, and they couldn't bend over at the waist to decrease the size of the target they offered. Because of that, and because their mission was no longer a surprise, they were easy targets for the Indians, who concentrated all their fire on the four men.

All four were hit, and when two of them, Bailey and Glass, went down, Jacob could tell even from where he was that they were dead. That left Corn and Moore wounded, each of them now alone with their burdens. They continued on, despite their wounds and the weight of the water barrels they were carrying.

Without giving it a second thought, Jacob crawled up from the ravine and ran toward Corn, taking the barrel from him.

"You help Moore!" he said, and though wounded, the two of them were able to get the water barrel the remaining few yards. Jacob made it back with the water without being hit.

The three men were cheered mightily when they returned to the ravine.

THROUGHOUT THE REST of the day, the Rangers managed to hold off the Indians. Finally, darkness fell, and the shooting stopped.

"Major, we could more 'n likely get out of here now," one of the men suggested.

"How are we going to do that, Ranger Simmons? More than half of our horses have been killed, and Corn and Moore are wounded. Or do you propose to leave Corn and Moore behind?"

"No, sir, I damn sure wouldn't want to do that."

"What I need is a volunteer to go to Fort Richardson and report on our condition," Major Jones said.

"I'll go," Jacob volunteered. "I'll need a horse."

"You can take mine, Jacob," Corn offered. "That horse knows the way. All you gotta do is just get 'im pointed in the right direction, 'n he'll take you there."

Jacob started riding through the night, reaching the fort, which was adjacent to the town of Jacksboro, just before midnight. He was challenged by a sentry as he approached the gate.

"Who goes there?"

"Jacob Harrison. I'm a Texas Ranger, and my company is pinned down by Indians. Major Jones sent me here to ask for help."

"Wait here for a moment, sir," the sentry replied. Then he called, "Sergeant of the Guard, post number one!"

The sentry's call was repeated, and a short time later, another soldier appeared from the dark. Jacob gave him the same information he had given the gate guard.

No MORE THAN half an hour later, Jacob was leading a troop of the 10th Cavalry buffalo soldiers back to the valley were Major Jones and the Texas Rangers were waiting. Jacob thought it interesting that there wasn't an officer with the troop, it being led by Sergeant Major James Wilbur.

"Sergeant Major, hold up while I let the major know we're coming in," Jacob said.

Sergeant Major Wilbur called his troopers to a halt as Jacob drew his pistol. He fired one shot into the air, waited for a second, then fired two more. The signal was answered by two shots, a short break, then one shot.

The buffalo soldiers moved into position, and at dawn, they and the Texas Rangers went on the offensive, only to discover that during the night, the Indians had all withdrawn.

The bodies of Bailey and Glass were wrapped in blankets and returned to Fort Richardson, where the two Rangers were buried. Corn and Moore were taken to the post hospital, where they were treated for their wounds.

Major Jones gave his report to the post commandant.

"The Indians were equipped with Winchesters and Henrys, and there didn't seem to be any shortage of ammunition."

"How many were there?" Colonel Kirby asked.

"When we went into the valley, we thought we were in pursuit of no more than thirty, but there were many more on the high ground. I have no way of knowing, of course, but my guess is there were at least another fifty."

"And you say they were all gone this morning?"

"Yes, sir. I'm certain they knew your men had arrived, and they decided it would be best for them to withdraw. I want to thank you, Colonel, for sending your men to our relief, and I want to commend Sergeant Major Wilbur for his professionalism and leadership."

"Sergeant Major Wilbur is as fine a soldier as it has ever been my honor to command," Colonel Kirby said. "By rights, he should be a commissioned officer, but so far, the War Department has not seen fit to commission a colored man.

"Until they do, men like Sergeant Major Wilbur will continue to fulfill the jobs of officers."

ALTHOUGH FOUR MEN short of his original compliment, Major Jones left Fort Richardson the next day with fresh horses and proceeded north in search of more Indians. This time when Jacob went with them he was mounted, since Major Jones had been unable to get a replacement wagon.

Sergeant Major Wilbur and several of the buffalo soldiers turned out to bid them goodbye.

"Sergeant Major, are you sure you don't want to come with us?" Jacob asked.

"I'd come with you in a heartbeat, Ranger Harrison. In a heartbeat," Sergeant Major Wilbur said. "But the colonel says we'd best stay here for now."

"Sergeant Major Wilbur is a good soldier. I wouldn't mind ridin' with a man like that, even bein' that he's colored," Ranger Bivens said as the Rangers left the post. Bivens was riding alongside Jacob.

"He's a fine soldier," Jacob agreed.

3

Fort Dodge

THE SHOOTING EXHIBITION CAME A FEW DAYS AFTER CADE HAD officially become a scout. With almost the entire post gathered, the buffalo hunters, using their Sharps .50 caliber rifles that the men called the "Big 50", were asked to put on a demonstration. The marksmen routinely hit their targets at five hundred yards, then Joe Plummer spoke up.

"I think this business of Dixon and McCall makin' fifteen-hundred-yard shots is a bunch of bull. If they really can make a killing shot from fifteen hundred yards, I'd like to see it."

"Well, Joe, you could always go out there about fifteen hundred yards and let them take a shot at you," Bat Masterson suggested. Not only the other scouts but the gathered soldiers laughed at Bat's comment.

"I have a suggestion," Lieutenant Baldwin said. "Suppose we take a door from some structure, draw the outline of a man on it, stand it up fifteen hundred yards away, and let each man shoot at it?"

"Yeah," the farrier sergeant said. "Smith, you 'n Ellison go take that side door off the livery 'n bring it here."

Half an hour later, the door, with the outline of a man painted on it, had been stood up fifteen hundred yards from the firing line.

"You go first, Cade," Billy said. "Age before beauty."

The others laughed.

Cade took a prone position, aimed, and fired.

"Someone needs to check it out, because if there's only one hit, we won't know who it was," Lieutenant Baldwin requested.

"That won't be necessary, Lieutenant," Billy said as he got into position. "Cade didn't miss, and neither will I."

A moment later, Billy fired.

"I'll go check it out," Private Bledsoe said, mounting his horse and riding the near-mile out to the target.

Everyone waited patiently while Bledsoe covered the distance. He returned at a gallop, and when he dismounted, he was wearing a huge smile. "Two hits!" he called out excitedly. "Both of 'em right where the heart would be.

ON THE NIGHT before the troops were scheduled to depart Fort Dodge, a dance was held in the Sutler Store. The dance began at seven o'clock in a room that was decorated with banners, flags, and pennants. The brass buttons of the dress uniforms of both officers and men sparkled no less than the gold and jewelry that glittered on the necks and ears of the women of the post.

There were many more men than women, the only women present being the officers' ladies, the enlisted men's wives, and the few single laundresses. These events often found the women exhausted by the end of the evening because they were expected to dance with as many men as they could. Only Amy, the sixteen-year-old daughter of the sutler, was young enough and excited enough to show no diminution of energy.

Cade danced with Elizabeth Powell, the surgeon's wife, Juanita, the wife of Sergeant Flynn, who was one of the laundresses, and young Amy.

"Why aren't you wearing your uniform?" Amy asked. "Why, I don't even know if you're an officer or an enlisted man."

"They won't let me wear my uniform," Cade replied.

"Why not? Did you do something wrong?"

"As far as everyone here is concerned, I fought for the wrong army. My uniform was gray."

"Oh! You mean you're a Rebel?"

"I was, but now I'm a scout for the soldiers in blue."

"Oh, *that's* why you don't wear a uniform. You're like Mr. Chapman and Mr. Dixon. And Mr. Masterson. Isn't he the most handsome man you've ever seen?"

Cade shook his head. "Everybody loves Bat, that's for sure."

After the Grand March that concluded the dance, General Miles held an officers' call, which included Cade and all the scouts.

"I know you're aware that we'll soon be taking the field in pursuit of hostiles," Miles began. "Before I give you the specifics of our operation, I would like to share with you the overall plan as designed by Generals Sherman and Sheridan.

"Major William Price will leave from Fort Union, New Mexico Territory and head east across the Texas Panhandle with four companies of the 8th Cavalry. Lieutenant Colonel John W. Davidson will march southwest from Fort Sill with eight companies of the 11th Infantry, and Lieutenant Colonel George Buell will move northwest from Fort Griffin with seven companies of the 9th Cavalry. Colonel Ranald Mackenzie, with eight companies from the 4th Cavalry, and D Company from the 10th, will depart from Fort Richardson. Finally, we will leave Fort Dodge and head south. In total, it is expected that there will be some three thousand soldiers involved in the overall campaign. It is General Sheridan's strategy that a five-pronged pincer will converge in the Texas Panhandle like the spokes of a wagon wheel, and we will sweep the opposing forces into the headwaters of the Red River at the hub.

"General, will we be maintaining contact with all these other elements?" Lieutenant Baldwin asked.

General Miles nodded. "Yes, when possible, though I expect our closest coordination will be with Colonel Mackenzie. I have been given operational control of both my own and Mackenzie's commands. Accordingly, I will seek to establish communication with him at various times during the expedition.

"Now, as we will be leaving in the morning, I suggest you give your individual commands the information they will need, then get some rest."

All the officers present came to attention and saluted, then left the post headquarters to pass on such information as would be necessary for their subordinates to know.

"So, we're going down into the Panhandle. Somehow I get the idea that we'll be going back to Adobe Walls," Cade said as he, Billy, and Bat, returned to the barracks that had been provided for the white scouts.

"Yes, I was talking to Lieutenant Baldwin during the dance tonight," Bat replied. "He said that shortly after we leave here tomorrow, he and his scouts, meaning us, will be detached from Miles and the others. We're to scout west along the Beaver River all the way to the Palo Duro Creek tributary, then south to Adobe Walls. Lieutenant Henely will be coming with us."

"He's one of the scouts?" Billy asked.

"No, he'll be in command of a detail of sixteen troopers from the 6th Cavalry."

Billy nodded. "It'll be good to have them along."

"And it'll be good to go back to Adobe Walls and see who's still there," Cade added.

"I wonder if Hanrahan's still there?" Billy asked.

"Hanrahan? Or his saloon?" Bat asked.

"Well, yes, his saloon. I don't give a damn if he's actually there or not." Billy laughed. "But wouldn't it be good to have a beer after a long march, especially as hot and dry as it is now?"

"Yes, dry is the operative word," Bat agreed. "All of us have hunted all over this territory, and we all know the water situation. But in this drought, what good water there is will probably be dried up, and the water we do find is liable to be gyp water."

The bugle call of *Tattoo* drifted across the post, which signaled all to return to quarters since there were only thirty minutes until lights out.

For the next half hour, the men spoke quietly until the haunting sound of *Taps* signaled it was time for bed.

"Post number one, ten o'clock, and all is well!" a guard called.

"Post number two, ten o'clock, and all is well!"

The calls continued in Doppler effect—faint, louder, loud, then fading once again until faint at the last call. *"Post number twelve, and all is well!"*

THE NEXT MORNING eight companies of the 6th Cavalry and four companies of the 5th Infantry were turned out on the parade. The horses were still in the stables, so that the cavalrymen were standing in "dismounted drill" formation, along with their infantry brothers. Earlier, the signal cannon had marked the raising of the flag, and now over three hundred men stood at ease, with Major Biddle at their head.

The scouts, although present for the formation, were not part of it. Cade saw the door to the headquarters building open, and General Miles came walking toward the parade quadrangle, slapping a swagger stick against his thigh.

When Major Biddle saw the general, he came to attention.

"Regiment!" he called.

"Battalion!" shouted battalion commanders Major Compton and Captain Hugh, who was filling in for Major Biddle, giving the first of the supplemental commands.

"Company!" the company commanders called.

"Platoon!" the platoon leaders responded.

When all the supplemental commands had been issued, Major Biddle gave the final operative command.

"ATTEN-*SHUN!*"

General Miles stepped in front of Major Biddle and the major saluted.

"Sir, the expedition regiment is formed and ready!"

Miles returned the salute.

"Officers and men, you will be called to horse in one-half hour, at which time we will take to the field. Dismissed."

Upon being dismissed, those officers and non-commissioned officers who were married hurried to tell their wives and families goodbye before retrieving their horses. The stable was busy while the horses, most of which were already saddled, were led out to await their riders.

Lieutenant Henely and the men who would be with him had made the initial formation, but once they had their horses saddled, they reported to Lieutenant Baldwin instead of returning to the parade.

"We'll wait until the others have left the post, then we'll overtake them and scout on ahead," Lieutenant Baldwin said.

The bugler played *Assembly,* and the parade quickly filled again. This time the cavalrymen stood by their horses until ordered to mount. Then, with the band playing *The Girl I Left behind Me* and the general riding at their head, the body of men who would now be known as the Miles Expedition left Fort Dodge.

Those who were left behind—garrison soldiers who weren't part of the operation, civilian employees, and the women, including the soldiers' wives and their children—watched, some tearfully, as the men departed. Then a strange mirage occurred. A mist had gathered, so that as the regiment marched away, their exact mirror image was reflected in the sky above them.

"Oh, look, Mama, they are all going up to heaven," a little girl exclaimed.

"Sally, no! Don't say that!" the little girl's mother replied, frightened by the thought.

Except for the little girl's comment and her mother's response, the mirage brought about a strange, quiet foreboding among all who were back at the post. Even Lieutenant Baldwin's order a few minutes later was subdued.

"All right, gentlemen, we'll get underway now," he said.

By the time Baldwin and the others in his detail had left, the mist had lifted and the mirage was gone.

"At a trot," Baldwin ordered.

Within fifteen minutes, they had overtaken General Miles and his command and were proceeding on ahead.

4

Elgin, Kansas

WHILE STEPHEN GERMAN WAS PUTTING HAY IN THE TROUGH, HIS sister Rebecca was milking a cow. Joanna came into the barn and, with a toss of her long blonde hair, held out a handful of wildflowers she had just picked. She showed them to Stephen.

"Don't you think Mama will like these flowers?" she asked.

Stephen grinned at her. "Sure. Wouldn't *you* like them if some boy gave them to you?"

"What boy?"

"Oh, I don't know. Drew Emerson, maybe?" Stephen teased.

"Oh? Have you heard him say something?"

"It could be."

"What did he say? What did he say?"

"Oh, I'll never tell."

"Joanna, don't listen to him. He's just fooling with you," Rebecca said.

The girl pouted. "That's...that's not a very nice thing for you to do."

"No, it isn't," Rebecca chastised Stephen.

Stephen laughed. "I should have a brother. All six of my sisters gang up on me all the time."

"Well, if you weren't so mean, we wouldn't do it," Joanna said, brushing a lock of hair away.

Sophia came out to the barn from the house.

"Mama says to get washed up and come in for breakfast. Joanna, you'd better go find Julia and Addie," Sophia told her sister.

"I've been smelling the bacon cooking all morning, and it's making me hungry," Stephen said.

"Oh, pooh. When are you *not* hungry?" Rebecca asked, picking up the pail of milk.

"Here, let me carry that," Stephen offered, reaching out to take it from her. As they approached the house, Catherine stepped onto the back porch and poured out a dishpan of dirty water.

"Have you been helping Ma cook? I probably won't be able to eat, then," Stephen teased.

"That'll be the day," Catherine shot back.

A few minutes later, with his entire family gathered around the table, John German gave the blessing as his wife Lydia and all seven of their children bowed their heads reverently.

"Papa, did you see the flowers I picked for Mama?" Joanna asked.

"How can I not see them, child? They're sittin' there right in the middle of the table," John replied.

"That's where they should be, because I think they're very pretty," Lydia said.

Stephen finished eating first, but when he started to get up, John held his hand out in a motion for him to remain.

"Don't leave yet," John said.

"I was goin' to tighten up the shear on the plow, Pa."

John shook his head. "There won't be no need for that."

Stephen chuckled. "Pa, you can't plow with a broken shear."

"We won't be doin' any more plowin'. Leastwise, not here."

"John, what are you talkin' about?" Lydia asked.

"I think you know the answer to your question," John replied.

Lydia sighed and nodded. "I think I do."

"Yesterday, I traded for another cow, two calves, ten hens, and two roosters. We'll be takin' them with us. Lydia, children, I've made a decision. We're going to do what I've always intended for us to do. We're going to Colorado, and I want to be there for the spring plowin'. We'll be needin' to get started right away if we're goin' to get there before the snow flies."

"Good!" Stephen said.

"Oh, Papa, must we?" Rebecca asked. "We were in Tennessee, we were in Missouri, and now we're in Kansas. I thought we were going to settle down here? I mean, we have such a lovely farm."

"Rebecca, I've always wanted to go to Colorado. You complain about all the moving? Well, I would have gone there directly from Georgia if we could have, but it cost too much, so we've had to work our way across the country in stages. There's only one more move we have to make, and this one will be the last one, I promise you. Now, what do the rest of you say?"

"If that's what you've always wanted to do, then who are we to say otherwise?" Catherine asked. "I'm ready to go."

John patted his daughter's hand.

"How far will we have to walk?" Addie asked. "I get tired if I have to walk too far."

Stephen laughed. "Don't worry, little one. If you get too tired, I'll sweep you up and put you on my shoulders."

"Oh, yes! I would like that!" Addie squealed with delight.

"Lydia, we haven't heard from you."

"You are my husband, John. Wherever you go, I will go as well."

John hugged Lydia. "You know, I'm glad I married you. I think I'll keep you around."

"Ain't it a little late to be changin' your mind?" Stephen asked with a little laugh.

SHORTLY AFTER MAKING arrangements to sell his farm and buy a wagon and a team of oxen, the German family started their trip, stopping first in the little town of Elgin to take on supplies. John bought powder and shot for his rifle, a Springfield 1861 model, which was the same kind of muzzleloader he had used during the war. He also bought some tools he was sure he would need—an axe, a saw, a hammer, and some nails. He left the rest of the shopping to Lydia, Rebecca, and the girls while he and Stephen went into the Elgin Saloon.

"We'll have a beer," John said.

"John, is it true you're plannin' on movin' to Colorado?" the bartender asked.

"Yeah, it's true. We'll be headin' out today. Right now, in fact, or at least as soon as the women can get their shoppin' done," John replied.

"I hate to see that. We're sure goin' to miss you around here."

"Ward, for as long as you've known me, you've known I've had it in mind to go on out to Colorado," John said.

"Yeah, well, lots of folks make plans. They just don't that many of 'em actual go on 'n do what they say they're plannin' on doin'."

"Here's one that'll do what he says he's goin' to do," John said, pointing to his chest with his thumb. "I've been workin' my way west ever since I got out of that Yankee prison camp."

"Well, seein' as you'll be leavin' for Colorado soon 'n this will more 'n likely be your last beer for a while, these two for you 'n your boy is on the house," the bartender said as he filled two mugs and set them before John and Stephen.

"Thank you, Ward. That's real good of you," John replied.

"So, John, you're goin' to Colorado, are you?" one of the other saloon customers asked.

"I am indeed. I guess that means you're going to have to find someone other than me to beat you in horseshoes."

"Hell, John, it ain't goin' to be that hard for 'im to do that, seein' as there ain't hardly nobody around who can't beat Sam at horseshoes," another said to general laughter.

"How is it that you're a' plannin' on goin'?" Sam asked.

"What do you mean, how am I goin'? I done bought me a good sturdy wagon 'n a pair o' strong oxen."

"No, what I mean is, what route are you a' takin' to get there?"

"I figure on followin' the Union Pacific Railroad. That way there ain't no way we can get lost."

Sam shook his head. "You don't want to go that way."

"Why not?"

"Maybe you ain't noticed, but we're right 'n the middle of a drought, 'n if you follow the railroad, there ain't no water."

"What do you mean, there ain't no water? There's got to be water in the stations, 'cause the trains need water to run," John stated.

"That's just it. The trains need water, 'n when there's a drought like this 'n we're a' havin' now, the station attendants won't let you have none o' their'n. If I was you, I'd go by way of the Santa Fe Trail. You can't get lost that way neither, 'n there's plenty o' creeks 'n rivers 'n such for you to get water. Hell, you'll practically be followin' the Beaver River."

"What do you think, Pa?" Stephen asked.

"Well, your ma 'n the girls ain't goin' to like it, on account of we prob'ly won't come through as many towns. But Sam's right; we're goin' to be needin' water, so we'll have to go where we can find it."

"I don't figure they'll make too big a fuss," Stephen said. "They'll be usin' more water than we will, what with the cookin' 'n the washin' 'n such."

"What about the Indians?" Ward asked.

"What Indians?"

"Ain't you been readin' nothin' at all in the papers?" Ward asked.

"I don't get no paper, so I don't know what you're talkin' about."

"Well, sir, there's just been all kinds of Indian trouble here lately. First there was that fight at a place called Adobe Walls. Then there's been some buffalo hunters that's been kilt. If I was you, I'd do what you was plannin' on doin' in the first place, 'n that would be to follow the railroad track. There's almost always people around the track, 'n the Indians ain't likely to get that far north."

"Where is this place, Adobe Walls, you're talkin' about?" John asked.

"It's down in Texas," Ward told him.

"And the buffalo huntin'?"

"Well, that's mostly goin' on down in Texas too, though some of it is in the Territories," Ward admitted.

John smiled. "Well then, since we ain't a' plannin' on goin' through Texas or the Territories, 'n since we ain't goin' to be doin' no buffalo huntin', I can't see as how we'll be havin' any kind of a problem. And the way I'm lookin' at it, we can either go along the track and do without Indians while we're dyin' of thirst, or we could go the way Sam suggested where there's plenty of water, 'n any Indians as we might need to worry about are more 'n likely down in Texas. I chose to go where there's water."

Ward smiled. "You're prob'ly right, I just thought I would tell you, is all."

Later, after they had left the saloon and started toward the wagon, John spoke to his son.

"Stephen, don't you be sayin' nothin' 'bout Indians to your ma 'n the girls. They ain't no sense in causin' them no worry about it."

"I won't, Pa," Stephen promised. "I won't say one word about it."

When John and Stephen reached the mercantile, they found Lydia and all the girls ready to go except Joanna.

"Where's Joanna?" John asked.

"I don't know," Lydia said. "She was standing right here by the wagon not more than ten minutes ago. I've been looking for her."

"Girls, do any of you know where your sister is?" John asked.

"She told me not to tell," Addie said.

"Addie, where is she?" Lydia asked.

"I'll get in trouble with her if I tell."

"Young lady, you will get in trouble with me if you *don't* tell," Lydia said. "Now, who would you rather be in trouble with, me or your sister?"

"She's over there by the feed store, talkin' to her boyfriend."

"Boyfriend? What boyfriend?" John asked.

"Drew Emerson," Catherine said.

"You don't have to go with them," Drew said. "You could stay here 'n live with us. I know Ma 'n Pa would let you stay."

Joanna shook her head and wiped the tears from her eyes. "No, my ma and pa would never let me do that. Anyway, I wouldn't want to. I couldn't stand to think I wouldn't ever see any of them again."

"That's how I'm feelin' right now, thinkin' about how I won't never see you no more neither."

"When you're older 'n can go somewhere by yourself, you could come out to Colorado and see me."

"Yeah," Drew agreed. "Yeah, that's what I'll do. I'll come out to Colorado, 'n me 'n you can get married. Promise me you won't marry nobody out there in Colorado."

Joanna chuckled through her tears. "How can I marry somebody in Colorado when I don't know nobody in Colorado? Besides, I'm only fifteen years old. Pa says that's not old enough to get married."

Drew smiled. "Good, then me 'n you's promised to one another until you're old enough."

"Joanna, you'd better come on," Catherine called. "Pa's ready for us to leave."

Joanna turned to go but Drew put his hand on her shoulder. "Promise me you'll write?"

"I promise," Joanna said. She started to leave, then turned back and, to Drew's surprise, gave him a quick kiss. Then, embarrassed, she ran to join her older sister.

Lydia, along with the two youngest children, Julia and Addie, was on the wagon seat. John, Stephen, Rebecca, and Sophia were standing alongside.

"All right," John said as Joanna and Catherine arrived. "Lydia, get 'em goin'."

"Heeh-ya," Lydia called as she snapped the reins of the ox team. The wagon started forward.

"Good luck, John! Lydia!" someone shouted, and by the time the wagon had rolled out of town, nearly a dozen others had either called their greetings or come out into the street to walk with them.

Drew Emerson was one of those who came to walk with them, or more specifically, to walk with Joanna, and he stayed with her until they were at least a mile out of town.

"I've...I've got to go back now, Joanna," Drew said. "I been neglectin' my work, 'n Pa will be mighty vexed."

"Bye, Drew," Joanna said.

After Drew left, Joanna walked alongside the wagon while tears slid down her cheeks.

Lydia was aware that Joanna was crying. She wasn't sure what to say to her, but she felt she should say something.

"Girls, crawl in the back and make room for Joanna to ride up here with me."

The girls complied, and Lydia stopped the wagon. "Come up here and sit by me for a while," she said, patting the seat beside her.

Using the front wheel spokes as steps, Joanna climbed into the wagon. Once she was seated, Lydia snapped the reins, and the oxen got started again.

"Drew is a nice boy."

"We're goin' to get married," Joanna told her.

"When?"

"When we're old enough."

Lydia smiled. She was glad Joanna wasn't making any immediate plans.

5

ON THE BEAVER RIVER

"IT'S NOT A VERY BIG RIVER," Lydia said. Although Lydia, Rebecca, and Catherine had been trading off the task of driving the wagon, Lydia was at the reins now, and the others were walking alongside.

John was on horseback, and although he normally ranged about, checking their route or keeping an eye on the cattle, at the moment, he was riding close enough to Lydia to engage her in conversation.

"Well, just how much water can you drink?" John asked, responding to her comment about the river.

Lydia laughed. "Not all that much, I reckon. But I do wish we had decided to follow the railroad."

"Why would you want to follow the railroad?"

"It's just, this is so... Well, I can't think of the word, but there are no people here."

"The word is 'isolated,'" Rebecca said. She was walking close enough to monitor the conversation.

"Yes, isolated. John, don't you think it would be better if we could see some people every now and then?"

"I admit it might be nice to see someone ever' so often, but as hot as it is, and what with the drought 'n all, it's a lot better to have water close by. You've never been really thirsty, but I have. Sometimes the Yankee guards at Douglass would keep us prisoners under control by rationing the water."

"Papa, you were a prisoner?" Addie asked.

"Yes, darlin', I was."

"Why were you a prisoner? Did you do something wrong?"

"No, sweetheart, your papa didn't do anything wrong," Lydia said. "He was in the war, and he was captured by the enemy."

"What does 'captured' mean?" Addie asked.

"It means when someone takes you away and keeps you from being with the people you love, like your family and friends," Lydia explained.

"Oh, I wouldn't want to be captured," Addie exclaimed, the tone of her voice reflecting her fear of such a situation.

"Joanna has been captured," Catherine teased. "She's been captured by Drew Emerson."

"I plan to capture someone someday," Stephen said, "soon as I find me a woman pretty enough for me to marry, 'n who's willin' to do ever' thing I tell her to."

"So, you think taking a wife is the same as takin' someone on to work for you?" Rebecca asked.

"Well, ain't it?"

"If you think that way, I'm goin' to tell every woman you ever meet to run away from you," Rebecca said with a laugh.

"Shh! Stop the wagon," John said, holding up his hand. "Lydia, hand me down my rifle."

"What is it?" Lydia asked anxiously.

"I just seen a deer behind them trees. I figure we can be eatin' off him for the next three or four days."

With Lieutenant Baldwin's scouts

AT THAT VERY MOMENT, a few miles northwest of the German wagon, Lieutenant Baldwin, Cade, Billy, Bat, and the scouts, as well as Lieutenant Henely and the troopers who were with them, were headed south on their way to the Beaver River, having crossed the Arkansas.

"Mr. McCall, Mr. Masterson, I would like for the two of you to be the advance party. I want you to scout ahead for about a mile, and if you encounter any hostiles, return quickly and alert us."

Cade nodded, then he and Bat went on ahead. They rode in silence, not wanting to make their presence known to the Indians through careless conversation. After a while they split up, with Bat scouting out to the west and Cade to the east.

Half an hour after they had separated, Bat rode back with a concerned look on his face.

"Bat, what'd you find?"

"Come with me," Bat said without further explanation.

Bat led Cade through the trees and across a ravine to Crooked Creek. When they reached the creek, the reason for the serious look on Bat's face became apparent. Here, at what had obviously been a campsite, were what remained of five men.

"Damn," Cade said. "I've seen battlefields that looked better than this."

All five men had been scalped and their heads were bashed in, so that their brains had spilled out. There were also bloody gashes on their bodies, and every one of the bodies had arrows protruding from it. The wagon had been burned, and the oxen killed. Also killed was a dog, which, poignantly, was lying with its head on the leg of one of the men.

"These men don't look like buffalo hunters," Bat said. "I wonder what the hell they were doing out here."

"This will answer your question," Cade said, pointing to a tripod-mounted device lying on the ground. "That's a transit. These men were surveyors, probably laying out the route for a new railroad."

"The railroads are going everywhere, springing up like spider webs. You can hardly blame the Indians for getting a mite peevish.

The time will come, and relatively soon, where you won't be able to throw a stick without hitting a white man."

"We'd better go back and report to Lieutenant Baldwin. He's going to need to see this before we bury these poor souls," Cade suggested.

"WHY THE HELL do we need to bury 'em?" Joe Plummer asked when the rest of the men had been brought up.

"Don't you think their families might take some comfort in knowing they were at least buried?" Billy Dixon asked.

"What families?" Plummer asked. He took in, with a wave of his hand, the bodies which had now been moved into a single line preparatory to burial. "We don't even know these sumbitches' names, so how the hell are their families ever goin' to find out about 'em?"

"Plummer, you'll take your turn at the shovel just like everyone else," Lieutenant Baldwin said.

"What are we goin' to do with the dog, Lieutenant?" Amos Chapman asked. "I mean, you said you plan to leave the oxen where they are, but I think we should bury the dog."

"I ain't diggin' no hole just for a damn dog," Plummer complained.

"We don't need an extra hole," Chapman said. He pointed to one of the bodies. "The dog was lyin' with his head on this man's leg, so I'd be thinkin' it was his dog. We should bury 'em together."

Baldwin nodded. "Good idea, Amos."

Once the five surveyors were buried, Baldwin decided they would camp here on Crooked Creek for the night.

After tethering their horses, and putting out sentries, the rest of the men settled down around a campfire and ate their supper of beans and bacon.

"I tell you what," Ben Clark said, who was one of the white scouts. "If ever I needed a reason to kill me a bunch of Indian bastards, what we saw today is reason enough."

"There are those in the East who don't agree with what we're doing out here," Lieutenant Henely said.

"What do you mean?" Billy asked.

"Oh, the press writes glowing accounts of the poor Indians and their mistreatment at the hands of the white man. They subscribe to the words of the poem by Alexander Pope."

"What poem is that?" Baldwin asked.

"Well, I can only remember the first two lines, but it is *Lo, the poor Indian! whose untutor'd mind, Sees God in clouds, or hears him in the wind.*"

"So that's where it comes from!" Amos Chapman said, slapping his knee. "I was with Custer at Washita, 'n he 'n the other officers with him kept calling the Indian's 'Lo.' I didn't know what they was talking about."

"Yes," Bat agreed, "I've heard that word used. 'Lo' has become a sarcastic pejorative meant to belittle people who pamper the 'noble' red man."

"It's become a what?" one of the others asked.

"A sarcastic pejorative, a way of making fun of those in the East who would mollycoddle the Indian," Bat explained.

"I don't hardly never unnerstand nothin' you ever say 'cause you say it in all that high-falutin' kind of talk," Plummer complained.

As they were talking, a lightning bolt split the night sky, followed quickly by a loud roar of thunder.

"Lieutenant, we'd better get to the horses," Cade warned. "If there's a thunderstorm coming up, we'll have a hard time keeping them from running off."

"You're right," Baldwin said, "and this is going to take all of us. Turn out, turn out, every man!"

The scouts, white and Indian, and every trooper in Henely's command started toward the horses.

Plummer didn't respond to Baldwin's order.

"Plummer, didn't you hear me?" Baldwin called to him.

"I signed on to scout, not tend horses," Plummer replied.

"Get out there *now*!" Baldwin demanded, anger evident in his voice.

"All right, I'm a-goin', I'm a-goin'," Plummer whined.

Just as the man stood up, the rain started, not with a trickle but with a heavy downpour.

"Damn, now it's plum-out rainin'," Plumer complained.

"You aren't made of sugar, so you won't melt," Baldwin said. "Now get to your horse."

With the German family wagon

"OH, Mama, we're getting all wet," Addie said.

"Get in the middle of the wagon. The rain isn't coming through the canvas so it can't reach you there."

"My pet chickens are getting wet."

"I've told you, Addie, don't make pets out of creatures we'll probably wind up eating," John said.

There was another streak of lightning and a rumble of thunder.

"How much longer do you think it'll be before we get there?" Catherine asked.

"You mean Colorado, daughter?"

"Yes, Papa, Colorado."

"About three more weeks, I'd say."

"That's a long time."

"Three weeks ain't nothin'. In the old days, when people went to California or Oregon, it would take them five or six months," Stephen said. "I read that in a book."

"Oh, the poor oxen! They're stuck out in this rain," Julia said.

"What about all the deer and buffalo and birds who live in the wild?" John asked. "They're always stuck out in the rain."

"I wish the rain would stop. I don't like it when it rains," Sophia complained.

"We've been in a drought, so it's good to have the rain," John said.

John's reply was punctuated by another loud peal of thunder. The family huddled together, uncomfortably crowded in the packed wagon. The rain continued until after midnight, then John and Stephen spread a large canvas sheet on the ground under the wagon and the two men, along with Lydia, Rebecca, Joanna, and Catherine crawled under the wagon to sleep the rest of the night. Sophia, Julia, and Addie slept inside.

"Oh, I like it the day after it's rained. Don't you, Mama? Everything smells so good," Addie said as the German family got underway the next morning.

Lydia laughed and ran her hand through Addie's hair. "Is this the same little girl who told me last night she didn't like the rain?"

"I don't like the rain, I just like the day after it's rained.

Catherine chuckled. "You can't have a day after the rain if you don't have the rain."

"Lydia, hold it up!" John called, putting his hand out.

Lydia pulled back on the reins, halting the oxen. "What is it, John?" she asked anxiously.

"I don't know. I just saw...oh, great! Never mind, it's the Army! There are soldiers ahead!"

Lydia slapped the reins against the backs of the oxen, and they resumed their slow, but steady plodding.

"Lieutenant, there's a wagon comin' this way," Amos Chapman said.

"Well, if it's a wagon, it isn't Indians," Henely added. The scouts and Henely's troops had just reached the Beaver River.

"With the Indians about, a wagon's got no business being out here like this, all alone," Billy stated.

"We'll wait for them," Baldwin said.

Cade and most of the others dismounted, taking the opportunity to relieve their horses of the burden of their weight. As the wagon drew closer, they saw one man riding a horse and five people walking

41

alongside the wagon, a young man and four girls. A woman was driving the wagon, and two smaller girls were riding on the seat with her.

The two men moved out ahead of the wagon with smiles and waves, drawing closer to the waiting soldiers.

"I'll be damned," Cade said softly.

"What is it?" Billy asked.

"I know that man."

"From Dodge? Who is he? I don't recognize him."

Cade didn't answer, but when the man came much closer, Cade called to him.

"John German," he said. "I never thought I'd see you again."

John dismounted and looked at Cade, clearly puzzled as to how Cade was able to call him by name. Then his face reflected recognition.

"McCall? Cade McCall?"

"That's me," Cade said, walking toward John with his hand extended. The two men shook hands heartily.

"You were part of the Forty- One Quad," John said.

"I'm surprised you remember," Cade said. "Working the crumb hole as you did, you saw just about every prisoner every day. It's easy for me to remember you. You were just one, but I was one of many."

"What in the h…" Billy started to say, but noticing the women and girls, he edited his comment. "What in the world are you two talking about?"

"We were both Confederate prisoners in Camp Douglass, the Yankee prison camp in Chicago," Cade said.

"'Forty-one quad?' 'Crumb hole?'"

"There were four of us who were good friends in barracks number forty-one, so we called ourselves the Forty-one Quad," Cade explained.

"And I worked in the kitchen, passing food through a window. The men called it the crumb hole."

"Like I said, John, you being the only one in the crumb hole, it's easy for me to remember you. Don't know how you were able to remember me, though."

"I remember your escape attempt," John replied. "Everyone remembers that, and how you almost made it."

"Yeah, almost," Cade said. "And we would have if we hadn't been betrayed."

"It was by one of your own too, wasn't it? A member of the Forty-one Quad?"

"It was Dolan," Cade said. "Albert Dolan. He not only betrayed us, but he also got a close friend killed."

"What do you think ever happened to him?" John asked.

"I killed him," Cade said without further explanation.

Cade's pronouncement was followed by a moment of silence, which was interrupted by Billy Dixon.

"Mr. German, if you don't mind my asking, what are you doing out here all alone?"

"We're on our way to Colorado," John replied, a big smile crossing his face.

"A single wagon filled with women... I don't mean to be rude or nothin', but this is hostile Indian territory, and you've got no business out here all by yourself. Why didn't you follow the railroad?"

"That was my original plan, but because of the drought, I was advised to come this way."

"You should have stuck with your original plan," Cade said. "If you would take my advice, you would turn north now and keep going until you run into the track. You should be able to make it to the railroad in no more than a week."

"We've been travelin' for two weeks now, 'n we ain't seen hide nor hair of an Indian. You're sayin' it would take me a week to reach the railroad, 'n the way you're tellin' it, I would still be in Indian territory for that whole week. But if I keep going the way I am, I'll reach Colorado in about two weeks, 'n that's just one more week extra."

"I think you should listen to your friend, Mr. German," Bat said.

"Let me ask you this…have you seen any hostile Indians?"

"We haven't seen any Indians," Bat admitted, "but we have seen some of the carnage they have wrought."

"Carnage?"

"We found a party of surveyors. All killed," Cade explained.

"But you didn't see the Indians who did it?" John asked.

"No."

"No, 'n you ain't likely to, neither," John said. "It seems to me that once they done somethin' like that, they'd more 'n likely run away to keep from gettin' caught. I figure our chances are just as good goin' straight on to Colorado as they would be goin' north to hit the rail-road. But, if y'all are plannin' on campin' here for the night 'n don't have no objections, we'll camp here too."

"I don't see any reason why you couldn't," Lieutenant Baldwin said, having joined the men long enough to overhear the conversation.

USING HER OWN FLOUR, sugar, and baking powder, supplemented by the supplies carried by scouts and soldiers, Lydia made a very large batch of sugar cookies. After supper, they all sat around the campfire, eating cookies, drinking coffee, and telling stories.

Cade and John exchanged stories about their time in the Yankee prisoner of war camp, Bat and Billy told about their experiences at Adobe Walls, and, at Billy's urging, Cade told about being shanghaied, then put on a ship for South America.

After all the stories were told, Lydia spoke to one of her daughters.

"Joanna, dear, why don't you get your guitar and sing for us?"

Joanna's long blonde hair glistened gold in the light of the camp-fire. Cade believed her to be about fourteen or fifteen. She was already a very pretty girl, and he was certain she would grow up to be a beau-tiful young woman.

Joanna could play the guitar very well, but what held the rapt attention of everyone present was the pure, sweet quality of her voice as she sang.

Oh, the years creep slowly by, Lorena,
The snow is on the ground again.
The sun's low down the sky, Lorena,
The frost gleams where the flow'rs have been

Cade could remember this song being sung around a hundred campfires during the war, but never had he heard it sung as movingly as it was by this lovely young girl.

Later, with all the cookies eaten, the coffee drunk, the stories told, and the songs sung, the last flickering flames of the fire burned out as Cade lay in his bedroll thinking of the evening. It had been an unexpected pleasure meeting an old acquaintance, and he was glad to see that John had such a fine family, but he couldn't help but feel some apprehension over John continuing along the path he'd chosen.

He wished John would turn north toward the railroad, but John's remark that to do so would just extend his time in danger for one additional week had some merit. Perhaps Cade's worries were all for naught.

6

After breakfast the next morning, Cade walked over to the German wagon as they were preparing to get underway. As it happened, it was Joanna who came to meet him.

"Have you come to tell Papa goodbye?" Joanna asked with a big smile.

"I have."

"He 'n Stephen are filling the water barrel. They'll be here in a minute."

"All right, I'll wait for them. By the way, Joanna, I thank you for singing for us last night. All the men enjoyed it very much."

"I'm glad they did. I like to sing. Sometimes I..." Whatever Joanna was going to say fell away as she saw her father and brother coming up from the river.

"Oh, here they are," she said, pointing toward her father and brother as they approached, each carrying a water barrel.

"Hello, Cade," John said as he set the barrel on the wagon's side shelf and began lashing it down securely with rope. "Come to tell me goodbye, have you?"

"Yes. John, I'm not going to try and convince you to go north to join the railroad, but I *am* going to tell you to keep your eyes open."

"Oh, we shouldn't have any trouble on that score," John replied with a little laugh. "After all, we have eighteen eyes to keep a lookout."

Cade laughed as well. "Yes, I guess you do." He reached out to take John's hand. "Be careful, my friend."

John watched the German wagon leave, heading not north toward the railroad track but west toward Colorado. His musing was interrupted by a shout from Lieutenant Baldwin.

"All right, men, let's move out," Baldwin called.

"FRANK, if we go riding in as one big group, isn't it possible that the men in the Walls might think we're Indians?" Lieutenant Henely asked, asserting his privilege to call a fellow officer by his first name. "It might be a good idea to send McCall, Masterson, and Dixon on ahead since they know most of the men who might be there."

"That's a damn good idea," Lieutenant Baldwin said as he turned to the scouts. "Dixon, you and McCall and Masterson go on ahead and tell anyone who might be a little trigger happy not to shoot us."

"Lieutenant, do you mean, don't shoot anyone? Or could they shoot someone if they chose the right person?" Billy asked.

"I would rather they not shoot anyone at all," Baldwin said, chuckling as he recognized Billy's comment for the joke it was meant to be. He was referring to Plummer, who had made an enemy of just about everyone in the patrol.

"All right. Cade, Bat, you heard the man. Let's pay a visit to some old friends," Billy said.

The three men, all of whom were veterans of the Battle of Adobe Walls, rode away from the bivouac.

As THEY RODE toward The Walls, Cade recalled the battle less than three months earlier. It was now being referred to as a "battle" even though not one soldier had participated in the engagement.

It had begun when James Hanrahan, the saloon owner, awakened the camp by firing a gun, then telling the others the sound had come from a ridgepole that had cracked. Hanrahan did it because Amos Chapman had warned him about the attack in advance, but the saloon owner hadn't told anyone about it since he was afraid the buffalo hunters might leave the compound, thus weakening their defense.

As a result of Hanrahan's action, most of the men were already awake and up at dawn when a combined force of Comanche, Cheyenne, and Kiowa warriors attacked them. There were at least seven hundred warriors armed with guns and lances and carrying heavy shields of thick buffalo hide.

Eleven of the defenders were in the Meyer and Leonard's store when the attack came, seven were in Rath and Wright's store, and ten were in Hanrahan's saloon. The three men who were now riding toward The Walls to tell them of the approaching soldiers had themselves been a part of the twenty-eight defenders, specifically the saloon contingent.

The Indians' initial attack was almost successful, as they got close enough to pound on the doors and windows of the buildings with their rifle butts. Although many of the defenders were buffalo hunters who were expert shots, initially the fight was in such close quarters that their long-range rifles were ineffective.

The Indians made repeated attacks, losing several of their own each time they did so. Then, after prolonged fighting had not given them their expected victory, the Indians withdrew to almost a mile away, trying to decide what to do next.

"Cade, let's take a shot at them," Billy Dixon had suggested.

"They're a long way off," Cade said. "Almost a mile, I would say."

"Well, these Big 50s have the range. If we don't hit any of them, we can at least ruffle their feathers a bit."

Cade chuckled. "All right, why not?"

The two men fired simultaneously, and their targets, two of the most gaudily-feathered Indians, went down. Upon seeing they could be killed at such a long range, the remaining Indians broke off the attack.

By the time the "battle" was over, the hunters had suffered four fatalities, three on the first day. The two Shadler brothers, who were asleep in their wagon, were killed in the initial onslaught, and Billy Tyler, who was shot through the lungs as he entered the doorway of a building while retreating from the stockade.

The fourth casualty was a tragic accident. On the fifth day, William Olds inadvertently shot himself in the head while descending a ladder at Rath's store.

All of this had been only a brief time before now, and while many of the original defenders of Adobe Walls had since left, there were still enough men remaining that anyone approaching the compound, whether they be Indian or white, would do so at their peril.

"You think they'll recognize us or start taking pot-shots at us?" Bat asked.

"I think as soon as they recognize us as white men, they'll let us get close enough to see what we want," Billy replied.

"If they recognize us as white men, they'll recognize *us*," Cade added.

"Oh, hell, that's not good," Billy said. "Why, there's no tellin' how many people ole' Bat here has gotten mad at him. 'N if they start shootin' at him, they're liable to hit us too."

"Damn, now you've got me scared," Cade said, and all three men laughed.

"What the hell?" Billy said a little later as they closed the distance. His outburst was from the grisly sight that greeted them. There were at least fifteen decapitated Indian heads stuck on the tops of posts, high enough above the ground to be easily seen on approach.

"Cade? My word, is that you, old chap?"

"Hello, Charley, you cockeyed Brit," Cade called back to Charley Armitage. "Can we come in?"

"But of course you can, my good man."

"Yeah, you can, but them two ugly galoots with you can't," one of the other occupants of The Walls said, stepping outside to join Charley.

49

"Ha! Imagine Mike Welch calling someone else ugly," Bat replied.

"Never mind. Come on in, the three of you," Mike invited. "Come to hunt buff again?"

"No," Cade said. "We're scouting for the Army. They'll be coming in about dusk, and we're here to tell you not to start shooting when you see 'em."

"I'll bet you haven't had a beer since you left Fort Dodge, have you?" Ernst Huffmann asked. Huffmann was one of the buffalo hunters who had taken refuge in The Walls.

"No, we haven't. Does Hanrahan still have his saloon open?"

"Hanrahan ain't here no more, but he left a couple of kegs of beer in the saloon. Come on in and we'll have a beer together."

Over the next hour, Cade, Billy, and Bat visited with those who were staying here, most of whom had shared the dangers of the Indian attack with them. Armitage, Frenchie, Robinson, Huffmann, and Old Man Keeler were among them.

"We still get a few Injuns who want to give us a try ever' now 'n then," Huffmann said. "But I reckon you seen our little show out front, what with all them Injun heads we put up on posts."

"That's a little gruesome, isn't it?" Billy Dixon asked.

"Oh, I quite agree, my good man," Armitage said. "But although it may be macabre, it does seem to be effective. We've had no more organized attacks since the one we had while you lads were still here."

"Here comes the Army!" someone shouted from the lookout balcony. "No, wait a minute! Some o' them is Injuns!"

"It's all right," Cade said quickly. "They're Delaware Indians, and they're damn good trackers."

"Wave that lantern, Pete," Huffmann called up to him. "Let 'em know we see 'em 'n they won't have no trouble comin' in."

A few minutes later, with Lieutenant Henely and his troopers leading the way and approaching in precise columns of two, the soldiers, civilian scouts, and Indian trackers were welcomed into the compound.

. . .

IN A SETTLEMENT that consisted primarily of buffalo hunters, one thing in abundant supply was buffalo meat. Baldwin and his scouts, Henely and his troopers, and Fall Leaf and his Delaware trackers ate better that night than they had at any time since leaving Fort Dodge.

"Hey, Mr. McCall, would you point out to me where you 'n Dixon was when the two of you made them long shots?" Bledsoe asked. This was the same trooper who had been the guard at the gate when Cade had ridden into Fort Dodge a few days earlier.

"Sure, come on. I'll show you," Cade agreed.

With the German Wagon

"ARE you sure we're doing the right thing by going on to Colorado instead of heading north to the railroad like those soldiers and your friend suggested?" Lydia asked.

The entire family was sitting around a campfire eating a supper of deer, potatoes, and biscuits. The deer had been cooked the day it had been shot and warmed up for tonight's meal, and it tasted as good as it had the first night.

"Lydia, it would take us a week to get to the railroad, and then two more weeks to get to Colorado. The way we're going will get us to Colorado in just two weeks."

"But didn't your friend say we were in Indian territory?"

"He did, and he might be right, but look at it this way. Would you rather be three weeks in Indian territory or only two weeks?"

Lydia frowned for a moment, then smiled. "I suppose if you put it that way, it might make sense."

"And another thing to think about," Stephen said. "One of the soldiers told me we were only a few days from Fort Wallace. Do you think the Indians are going to be anywhere near a fort?"

Lydia smiled again. "I guess I worry too much. The good Lord has taken care of us on this trek for a lot of years, and I don't think He will forsake us now."

51

"We're almost out of deer meat," Julia said as she reached for the last morsel of warm meat. "What are we going to eat when it's all gone?"

"We could always eat bugs," John suggested.

"Eat bugs? Eww! I could never eat a bug," Julia told him.

"You would if you were hungry enough, and you knew what kind of bugs to eat," John said.

"And what kind of bug would that be?" Stephen asked.

"I'd say the best bug to eat would be a grasshopper," John replied as he brushed one off his leg. "Nobody would starve to death this year, that's for sure. I've never seen as many as there are around here."

"I just hope the grasshoppers ain't this bad in Colorado. It'll be hard to raise a good crop if they're out there too," Stephen said.

"Well, we won't have to worry about that until next year," Lydia assured them.

"Why are we talking about eating bugs, anyway?" Catherine asked. "When we eat all of this deer, Stephen can just go kill another one."

"That's me," Stephen said with a proud smile. "The great hunter."

"Joanna, dear, why don't you sing us a song?" Lydia asked.

"I'll get the guitar!" Julia offered.

"Be careful with it," Joanna cautioned.

When Joanna began to play, the whole family joined in by singing *Happy Birthday*.

"I do declare," John said. "I plum forgot it's my birthday."

"We didn't forget," Catherine said. "We even made a special dessert."

Lydia went to the fire and pulled the Dutch oven out of the coals. "The girls made an apple cobbler for your birthday. It's the last of the dried apples, but we won't need any more until we get to Colorado."

"What about *my* birthday?" Stephen asked. "If today is Papa's birthday, then my birthday will be in a couple of weeks. What will you make for me?"

"Silly. We'll be in Colorado by then, and Mama will make you a cake," Addie said. "It's been so long since I ate a piece of cake, I can't remember what it tastes like."

"Come, my little one, come and sit by your old papa."

"How old are you, Papa?" Addie asked.

"I'm forty-four."

"Forty-four? Ain't that awful old?"

"It's not *that* old," Lydia said. "You don't remember Grandpa German back in Georgia, but he's almost seventy years old."

"Will you get that old, Papa?"

"I hope so," John said. "Now let's be quiet and listen to Joanna sing."

For the next hour, the German family listened to the strumming of the guitar and the pure sweet voice of Joanna as she sang for them. When Addie fell asleep on John's shoulder, Lydia reached over and put a shawl over the sleeping child. Then she took John's hand in hers.

"You know what, John? We've made a wonderful family."

John squeezed her hand in agreement.

Joanna put the guitar down. "Someday Drew and I will have a family just like this."

"Oh, I hope you don't have a boy like Stephen," Catherine teased, and with a chuckle, Stephen reached over to run his hand through his sister's hair.

A gas bubble trapped in one of the logs in the fire popped. It was almost as loud as a gunshot, and it startled everyone. Then, realizing what it was, they all laughed.

"It's time to get to bed," John said as he rose to his feet, being careful not to wake Addie. "I want to—"

The entire family finished what he was going to say.

"*Get started by the break of dawn,*" they said in unison.

"Oh, I've said that before, have I?"

"Yes, John, you've said it before."

"Well, then you know that's just what I want to do."

7

Adobe Walls

WITH SO MANY PEOPLE AT THE COMPOUND, THE OCCUPANTS BECAME
more confident of their position and several of them ventured outside
the walls.

"Hey, Tobe," Huffmann called to Robinson. "You know them wild
plums down by the river? What do you say me 'n you go gather us up
a bunch a them so's we can have us somethin' sweet to eat?"

"Yeah," Robinson said. "I could go for that."

"It's good of you boys to do that for us," Keeler said. "Some plums
would taste mighty good about now."

"'N we won't charge you no more 'n a penny apiece for 'em,
neither," Huffmann said.

"All right, it's worth it," Old Man Keeler said. "Since we have
plenty of sugar 'n flour, I'll make us up a plum cobbler."

"I don't know what the Army is out lookin' for," Mike Welch said
after Huffmann and Robinson left. "The Indians ain't really been both-
erin' us all that much, 'n when they do, well, we've took care of 'em.
I'm sure you seen them heads we got stuck up outside."

"They were hard to miss," Cade said.

54

"I have tried to explain to the gentlemen herein assembled that removing the head of your adversary is at best uncivilized, and at worst, barbaric," Armitage said in his crisp English accent.

"I quite agree," Bat said. "But Mike, as to your suggestion that the Indians are no longer active, I would like to point out an atrocity we came across on our way here."

Bat told of finding the slain and mutilated bodies of the five surveyors.

"I tell you who *I'm* worried about," Billy Dixon said. "On our way down here, we run across a family that was headed for Colorado all by themselves."

"How big a family?" Keeler asked.

"It was a pretty good-sized family. Two men, two women, 'n five little girls, it was," Billy answered.

"'N they was goin' by themselves?" Welch asked.

"Yes," Bat said. "I imagine Cade is the most concerned since he knew the family."

"To be clear, I didn't know the family. I only know John, and I knew him because we were in a Yankee prison camp together," Cade explained. "And since we weren't in the same barracks, I didn't actually have much interaction with him. Still, I wish we could have talked him into changing his route."

"Help! Help!"

The shout came from outside, and although there was no mistaking the urgency of the call, the volume of the shouting indicated that the person in danger was still some distance away.

"Damn if that don't sound like Huffmann!" Welch said.

Cade and the others rushed outside, where they saw two horsemen riding at top speed toward the Walls from the direction of the river. Ten or fifteen Indians were chasing them, and they made liberal use of their quirts on their ponies. They were doing their best to circle and cut off the two men in order to keep them from reaching the safety of the Walls.

Robinson and Huffmann were riding side by side and were able to maintain this position until they were rounding a little knoll just beyond the old ruins. Here an Indian who was mounted on an exceptionally fast horse managed to ride up near enough to run his lance through Huffmann's body.

"Son of a bitch!" Welch shouted. "They got Ernst!"

Huffmann fell, and his riderless horse continued running beside Robinson's. The Indian, who was still in pursuit, made repeated attempts to grab the rein of Huffmann's horse. Finally, he managed to get hold of it, then he turned around and rode back at full speed toward his companions with his prize in tow. All the Indians galloped away and disappeared among the sand hills.

The tragedy had happened so quickly that Cade could barely believe what he had just seen. The Indians had made no effort to mutilate or carry off Huffmann's body.

"Tobe, hurry,! Come on!" Welch shouted.

Robinson, still at a gallop, arrived in safety, although he was shaking with fear and exhaustion when he dismounted. Frenchie took his horse for him.

"What happened? Where did them Indians come from?" Welch asked.

"They was…" Robinson paused in his narrative to take several gasping breaths. "When we got to the river, the Indians was there, 'n they just sort of come on us before we could pick so much as one plum. Soon as we seen 'em, we jumped back on our horses to try 'n get back, 'n, well, you seen what happened."

"Troopers!" Lieutenant Henely called. "To horse!"

"We goin' after them heathen sons of bitches, Lieutenant?" Sergeant Willis asked.

"We are," Lieutenant Henely replied.

"Come on, men, you heard the lieutenant! Get mounted!" Sergeant Willis yelled.

Within a matter of minutes, the horses were saddled and, with Lieutenant Henely at their head, the troopers went in pursuit of the Indians.

"Tell me," Baldwin began, addressing Billy, Bat, and Cade, "you men are familiar with this area and with the habits of the Indians. Do you think Austin will find them?"

"Not a chance," Billy replied, shaking his head, and Bat and Cade agreed with him.

"Ernst was a good man," Robinson said. "Me 'n him has knowed each other for a long time."

"There's no need for his body to stay out there," Baldwin said.

"If somebody will go with me, I'll go bring 'im back in," Chapman said.

"I'll go with you," Welch offered. "I didn't know 'im as good as Tobe did, but I've knowed 'im for a while, 'n Huffmann was a damn good man."

"We can bury him next to those other four good men," Billy said, "Ike and Shorty Shadler, Billy Tyler, and Bill Olds."

"HEY, Jones, you was a preacher man once, 'n you said some words when we buried these other men," Welch said after the grave was dug. "Think you could say a few words for Ernst?"

"Ever'body, bow your heads real respectful," Jones requested.

To a man, they all removed their hats and bowed their heads.

"Lord, you heard what Tobe 'n Welch 'n some of the others said about Ernst Huffmann 'n how good a man he was, 'n I think so too. Also, you seen how ever'one turned out without complainin' to dig his grave. Now, like these other good people he's bein' buried alongside, our friend lies here, kilt by Godless heathens, so we're askin' that you take 'im into your bosom. Amen."

BY THE TIME they got the grave covered, they saw Lieutenant Henely and his troopers returning. Baldwin walked out to meet him.

"Did you find them, Austin?" Baldwin asked.

Henely shook his head. "No, they got away cleanly."

"Look here," Old Man Keeler said. "When is it you folks are plannin' on leavin'?"

"We'll be pulling out tomorrow morning," Lieutenant Baldwin answered.

"Then what I'm thinkin' is, when you folks leave, I'd like to go with you," Keeler said.

"Yeah, me too," Frenchie added. "I sure don't see no reason to stay here anymore."

"What do you think, Mr. Armitage?" Baldwin asked the Englishman. "Do you want to leave too?"

"After you leave here, do you have a particular destination in mind?" Armitage asked.

"We are to rendezvous with General Miles at Antelope Hills."

Armitage nodded. "Then I should like to go with you as well. I eventually want to go on to Camp Supply, but it would be comforting to have the Army as an escort for at least part of the way."

"All right, all of you can come with us, as long as you understand that I will be in charge. I know you are all civilians, but until we rejoin General Miles, you are under my command, just as you would be if you were soldiers. If any of you have a complaint about that, I would suggest you stay here."

"You'll get no complaints from me," Frenchie said.

"Nor from me," Armitage added.

"Hell, I ain't got none neither," Keeler said.

"Then when we leave, you gentlemen may go with us."

"You know what I'm thinkin'?" Billy Dixon asked. "I'm thinkin' this campaign will take care of the Indian problem down here once and for all."

"I think you're right," Chapman said. "With just about ever' soldier west of the Mississippi River on their tails, the Indians can't do nothin' but run."

Fort Richardson

When Jacob Harrison rode through the gate at Fort Richardson, he was recognized by the gate guard. The man had been one of the troopers who had come to the rescue of the Rangers when they had been pinned down in Lost Valley.

"Ranger Harrison," the gate guard greeted him with a broad smile. "You here to ask the D Troop to come save the Rangers again?"

"No, Booker, the Rangers sent me here to save D Troop," Jacob replied, matching Trooper Booker's smile. "May I come onto the post?"

"Yes, sir, come on in. Are you here to see the Sergeant Major?"

Jacob was actually there to meet with Colonel Ranald Mackenzie, but when he thought about it, he decided going through Sergeant Major Wilbur would be the proper thing to do.

"Yes, I am."

"Well, sir, you'll more 'n likely find 'im over in the post headquarters," Booker said.

Sergeant Major Wilbur was, as Booker had said, sitting at his desk in the post headquarters building, making some entries on a tablet. He looked up as Jacob approached.

"Ranger Harrison. What brings you here?"

"Hello, Sergeant Major. I have a note from Major Jones for Colonel Mackenzie."

"Do you want me to give it to him?"

"Actually, I would rather give it to him myself since the note involves me."

"All right, I'll see if the colonel is busy."

A moment later, Sergeant Major Wilbur came back. "He'll see you now."

Mackenzie was standing when Jacob went into his office, but he didn't offer his hand to shake. Jacob had been told that Mackenzie was very self-conscious about his hand. He'd had two fingers shot off his right hand during the war, and because of that, he was addressed by the Indians as "Bad Hand."

"Ranger, what can I do for you?" Mackenzie asked.

"This note will explain it, sir," Jacob said, handing him the note Major Jones had written.

COLONEL MACKENZIE, my respects, sir. It has been brought to my attention that you are requesting men from the Frontier Battalion of the Texas Rangers to serve as scouts with your detachment. It is with pleasure that I offer the services of a recent recruit, Jacob Harrison. Mr. Harrison was engaged in the freighting business prior to joining my company. I believe he will have much to offer, with his knowledge of the terrain and the added benefit of being a competent driver, should that be your most needed asset.

Respectfully,
John R. Jones
Major, Texas Rangers

Mackenzie looked up from the note. "How were you selected, Mr. Harrison?"

"I am the newest member of Major Jones' company," Jacob said, and then he smiled. "And besides that, I volunteered. I've read about your way of handling the Kickapoo on the Mexican border, and I respect that, sir."

"Don't believe everything you read, Ranger Harrison," Mackenzie stated, then called, "Sergeant Major, take this man to Captain Beaumont. He'll serve as a scout for tomorrow's expedition."

"Very good, sir," Sergeant Major Wilbur said as he stepped into the room.

"CAP'N BEAUMONT, sir, this is Ranger Jacob Harrison," Wilbur said.

"'Ranger?' Do you mean Texas Ranger?" Beaumont asked, directing the question toward Jacob rather than Wilbur.

"Yes, sir. I'm with the Texas Rangers."

"Why are you here? Is someone in my command in trouble with the law?"

"No, sir, nothing like that. I've been assigned to Colonel Mackenzie, and he is to use me any way he wishes. I believe the colonel has assigned me to your troop as a scout."

"As a scout. Do you know this country, Mr. Harrison?"

"Yes, sir, I do."

"Are you also aware that I am to leave on an expedition tomorrow morning?"

"Colonel Mackenzie said as much when he assigned me to your command."

"We have learned that Lone Wolf's band of Kiowas, strengthened by warriors from the Southern Cheyennes, Commanches, and Arapaho, have left their reservations to establish themselves somewhere within the breaks of the staked plains.

"Our orders are to intercept them, break up their camps and villages, and drive the Indians back to their reservations. We understand that these orders come directly from General Sheridan himself. We are to subjugate or, failing that, annihilate the hostiles. I trust you will have no trouble following those specific orders while you are riding with us?"

"No, sir, I will have no trouble with them."

"Good. We leave at dawn."

THOUGH THE HORIZON was somewhat lighter in the east, the sun had not yet risen as Jacob rode through the front gate of Fort Richardson with Captain Beaumont, Sergeant Major Wilbur, and one hundred troopers from D Troop of the 10th Cavalry.

8

Even as Jacob was setting out with Captain Beaumont, Cade, with Baldwin and his scouts and Henely and his troopers, as well as the buffalo hunters who had come with them from Adobe Walls, were rendezvousing with General Miles at Antelope Hills.

"Lieutenant, where did you pick up all these civilians?" General Miles asked.

"They're buffalo hunters, General. They were at Adobe Walls."

"Why are they with you now?"

"They asked us to provide escort for them until we were clear of the Walls," Baldwin said. "We witnessed the brutal attack and killing of one of their own right before our very eyes."

"I see," General Miles said. "And what are your plans for them?"

"They'll be going on from here, most of them to Camp Supply. They would like to bivouac with us tonight if you've no objections."

"I have no objections," General Miles replied.

"And one other item. I would like to dismiss one of my scouts, if I have your permission?"

"Would that be Plummer?"

"It is, sir. He is a constant source of discord among my men, as well as the scouts," Baldwin said. "He can move on with the buffalo hunters."

GENERAL MILES HAD with him eight troops of the 6th Cavalry, A,D,F,G,H,I, L, and M. The cavalry troops were arranged in two battalions, commanded by Major James Biddle and Major C.E. Compton, respectively. There were also four companies of the 5th Infantry under the command of Captain H.B. Bristol, and an artillery detachment commanded by Lieutenant James Pope.

Cade learned that Pope had brought some real firepower with him, to the tune of one breech-loading howitzer, a twenty-four-pounder, and two rather unusual guns that were unlike anything Cade had ever seen before. It appeared to be ten barrels in a circle.

Bat saw Cade examining the weapons.

"Gatling guns," Bat said without being asked. "Wait until you see them in operation. They are something to behold."

Cade shook his head. "They don't seem all that practical to me. I mean, even if you shoot all ten barrels at the same time, what is the real advantage?"

Bat chuckled. "There would be no advantage to that. But this," Bat pointed to a vertical shaft, "is filled with bullets. As you turn the crank," he pointed to the object, "it aligns one of the barrels with the firing pin. It shoots, then, as it rotates away, a spent cartridge is ejected from that barrel, and a new bullet is taken from this magazine and is ready to be fired by the next barrel. The faster you crank, the faster the gun shoots. You can shoot more than two hundred rounds in a minute."

"Damn!" Cade said. "I'm sure glad the Yankees didn't have anything like this during the war."

"They did have," Bat answered with a chuckle. "But fortunately for you, they didn't make much use of it."

"Bat, Cade," Billy said, approaching the two men. "Lieutenant Baldwin wants us."

"Yes, sir, what do you need?" Cade asked a moment later as the three men reported to the commander of the scouts.

"General Miles wants us to go on ahead," Baldwin said. "I've already told Fall Leaf. Get the others ready."

TWO DAYS LATER, one of the scouts came back from a brief patrol to render his report.

"There's something beyond that second ridge."

"Check it out, Lieutenant," Baldwin directed Henely.

"Sergeant Martell, with me," Henely said, dismounting and leaving his horse with the others along the slope. He and Martell advanced at a crouch to the crest. Once there, he leveled his field glasses for another look, then Sergeant Martell came down and made straight for Baldwin.

"Lieutenant Henely's compliments, sir, but there are a dozen Indians in sight, and he wishes to know, shall he charge?"

"A dozen Indians in plain sight?" Cade asked, having overheard the report. "That's strange."

"Quite strange," Bat Masterson agreed. "Normally they keep well out of sight, hiding behind sheltering crests and ridges in the open country or behind trees and underbrush when available."

"How far ahead are the Indians, Sergeant? Did you see them yourself?" Baldwin asked.

"Yes, sir, I seen 'em. It's real easy to see 'em. They're gathered up all in a bunch by the side of the road, jabbin' at somethin' on the ground with their lances."

"Mr. McCall, with me," Baldwin ordered, and the two of them followed the trooper back to the crest of the ridge. There they saw the Indians, who, as Sergeant Martell had reported, were poking their lances into something on the ground.

"They don't have any idea we're up here," Henely said. "For the whole time I've been here, they've done nothing but stick their lances into whatever that is on the ground. I fear it might be a white man."

"That doesn't seem right to me, Lieutenant," Cade said. "First of all, there's no way they haven't seen us. Secondly, they wouldn't all just stay in a bunch like that, knowing they could be seen from a ridge. And finally, if that is a white man on the ground, he would be dead by now, and they would have already scalped him."

"What do you think this is all about?" Baldwin asked.

"They want us to come charging down there, then they'll disappear. I expect there are a lot more Indians over that ridge than we have men with us."

Cade, Baldwin, and Henely watched for a while longer, then the Indians, possibly realizing their ruse had been discovered, disappeared over the next ridge. A few minutes later, some of the Indians began calling out to the soldiers and shooting. Not with any anticipation of actually hitting a target, but as a means of baiting the soldiers, in hopes of drawing them out.

Eventually, the Indians stopped their taunting and shooting. After at least an hour of quiet, Cade spoke up.

"I think they're gone."

"What makes you think that?"

"For one thing, we didn't take the bait, and for another thing, our position is tenable, theirs isn't. We have cover, food, and access to water. They don't. Sir, I'd like to go take a look."

"All right, go ahead. Take Dixon with you."

A few minutes later, Cade and Billy crossed the five hundred yards of open space, advancing one at a time. Cade would move forward for a hundred yards while Billy provided cover, then Cade would kneel, holding his Sharps .50 to his shoulder, watching the ground before them, and Billy would come up. In such a fashion, they covered the distance without incident. When they reached the bottom of the hill, they saw what the Indians had been poking with their lances lying on the ground.

"Hell of a way to treat a buffalo skin," Billy said, picking it up.

The two men advanced cautiously up the ridge, then looked over to the other side. There were no Indians there, but there was ample sign to show that they had been. Cade and Billy made a cautious but thorough investigation of the area, then returned to give their report.

"Nobody there," Billy said.

"How many were there, do you think?" Baldwin asked.

"I'd say at least five hundred," Cade replied.

"Five hundred?" Baldwin gave a little whistle. "I'm damn glad we didn't go off half-cocked after those few who were standing out there, trying to draw us in."

"Yeah," Henely said sheepishly. "I reckon I owe you boys my life, and not only my life, but the lives of all my men. Thanks for stopping me."

With the German Wagon

"OH, MAMA, I'M SO TIRED," Joanna said. "Can't I ride for a little while?"

"Would one of you girls like to get down so your sister can ride for a while?" Lydia asked.

"I'll walk," Addie offered. "If I get tired, Stephen will carry me on his shoulders," she added with a big smile.

"Don't you be bothering your brother," Lydia ordered as she stopped the wagon so the two girls could change positions.

"Mama, how old were you, when you and Daddy got married?" Joanna asked.

"I was seventeen."

Joanna smiled. "That's the same age as Catherine, which means I only have two years to wait, then Drew and I can get married."

"Sweetheart, I think you're going to have to just forget about Drew," Lydia said.

"Why? Me 'n Drew love each other."

"Because you are going to be in Colorado, and he will be in Kansas. You will be far apart, and you'll both be meeting new people."

Lydia smiled. "Why, a pretty girl like you will have so many beaus that your papa will have to beat them off with a stick."

Julia laughed. "Mama, would Papa really beat Joanna's beaus?"

"He won't have to," Joanna said, "because I will always love Drew, and I intend to be true to him."

AT THE END of a long day on the trail, not having seen another person, John called a halt for the night. Supper consisted of two rabbits Stephen had killed, after which the family sat around the fire, watching the golden sparks climb into the night sky to be lost among the stars.

"How far do you think we came today, Pa?" Stephen asked.

"Well, I reckon we were makin' about three miles to the hour, 'n we were underway for about ten hours, not countin' the times we halted, so, I'd say we made thirty miles, which was a pretty good day."

"Thirty miles in a whole day?" Rebecca said. "Why, you can go that far in one hour on a train."

"Could be," John replied with a chuckle. "Only thing is, we ain't on a train."

"I ain't never been on a train," Julia said, "but I'd sure like to go on one someday."

"You didn't carry me," Addie said to Stephen.

"What?"

"I walked today and I got tired, but you didn't carry me on your shoulders like you said you would."

Stephen stood up, then reached down to pick up his sister and lift her up to sit on his shoulders. Then, to the laughter of everyone, he began running around in circles, neighing like a horse.

Later that night, as the German family lay on blankets spread out on the ground next to the wagon, Sophia listened to her father's snoring and the soft breathing of her sister as sleep eluded her. Sophia had not been as openly opposed to their leaving as Joanna had been, but she too wished they had remained in Kansas. She didn't have a boyfriend like Joanna did, but she did have some friends she hated leaving behind.

It was no wonder Joanna had a boyfriend. She was the prettiest of all of them. Sophia wasn't jealous of her; she was proud of having a sister that was so pretty. Joanna was actually two years younger than Catherine, but she was a little taller, and well developed so most people who met them for the first time assumed that Joanna was the older of the two.

Some of her friends wanted to know what it was like to come from such a large family. Sophia was always a little surprised by the question and didn't know how to answer it. She loved her brother and all her sisters, and she couldn't imagine what it would be like to have a smaller family. Who would she give up in order to have a smaller family? Perhaps that was how she should have answered the question. She wouldn't give up anyone.

As she laid there, she listened to a chorus of howling coyotes, chirping crickets, and hooting owls. The ox team, as well as the two milk cows and two calves, could be heard chomping grass. This had become her regular nighttime symphony and, as it did every night, it lulled her to sleep.

9

COLONEL MACKENZIE HELD IN HIS HAND THE LETTER HE HAD JUST received from General Augur, Commander of the Department of Texas.

Colonel Mackenzie:

In addition to the troops already placed under your command, Colonel Buell has been instructed to support you with six companies of cavalry and two of infantry. You will also have within your command D Company of the 10th Cavalry.

As you are aware, General Miles, who is in joint command of both your forces and his own, is already in the field against the hostile Cheyenne, Comanche, Kiowa, and others who may have left their reservation. The purpose of the campaign is to punish them for their recent depredations along the Kansas and Texas frontiers, and you are expected to take such measures against them as will, in your judgment, soonest accomplish the purpose.

In carrying out your plans, you need pay no regard to Department or reservation lines. You are at liberty to follow the Indians wherever they go, even to the agencies. Should it happen in the course of the campaign that the Indians return to the agency at Fort Sill, you will follow them there and take such action as needed. While the Indian agent is to be consulted and treated with respect, he will not be permitted to interfere. You will answer only to this department or General Miles.

Supplies for your command will be sent to Fort Griffin until you suggest some other point. Make reports at every opportunity, and give as much detail as possible to General Miles.

Very respectfully,

C.C. Augur, Brigadier General

Commanding

"GENERAL MILES," Mackenzie said disgustedly as he slammed the letter down on his desk. "Miles may have been brevetted, but so was I, and now he and I are the same rank. I have as much right to be in overall command as he does. More even, since I am a graduate of West Point and he came up through the ranks in the volunteers. Now, because he's married to General Sherman's niece and General Sheridan has given him overall command, that...that *store clerk* will have a leg up on me for a brigadier general's star."

"'Store clerk,' Colonel?" Colonel Buell asked. The letter from General Augur had been delivered to Colonel Mackenzie by Colonel Buell.

"You mean you didn't know? While I was studying military tactics at West Point, Miles was selling yard goods in a store in Massachusetts."

"I didn't know that," Buell said.

"It isn't something Miles would particularly want anyone to know," Mackenzie said.

AT HIS OWN REQUEST, Jacob was with D Troop of the 10th Cavalry when Mackenzie's command left the post at 5:30 the next morning. They found no trace of the Indians on their first day out, and they continued for several more days with no signs, their biggest problem being a lack of water. Then, finding a freshwater spring, they bivouacked, filled their canteens, and prepared to move on the next day.

With General Miles

"I'M A LITTLE CONCERNED," Miles admitted to his officers. "If there are that many Indians ahead of us, we are outnumbered, and we are too far ahead of our train. We're desperately in need of water, the grasshoppers have eaten all the forage for the animals, and our ammunition is limited."

"What about the howitzer and the Gatling guns?" Lieutenant Baldwin asked.

"They aren't as mobile as we are, and they're at least a day behind us," Miles replied.

"General, with your permission, sir, I shall scout ahead so that we can locate the hostiles," Baldwin said.

"You won't be able to sneak up on them, Lieutenant," Miles said. "I don't think there's an Indian in Texas who doesn't know we're here."

"I'll be careful."

"Lieutenant Henely, you go with him."

"Yes, sir."

"General, I think my chances would be better if I didn't take a lot of men with me. If you don't mind, I think I want only Billy Dixon, Cade McCall, and Amos Chapman. We won't be as visible, and we won't make as much noise."

"All right, if that's how you want to do it."

"Be careful, Frank," Henely warned.

"I'll be as careful as I can."

Lieutenant Baldwin left his meeting with General Miles, then called Billy, Cade, and Amos to him.

"We're going to try and find the Indians," Baldwin said.

"Well, hell, Lieutenant, there ain't no tryin' to it," Amos said. "All we have to do is go about a mile south, stand there, 'n give a shout, 'n they'll find us."

Baldwin chuckled. "I've no doubt what you're saying is true, but I'd sort of like to find them on our terms. Oh, and because we are so short of water, we will take only two canteens for the four of us."

"Lieutenant, I can see one full canteen per two people, but we should all of us take a canteen, just have two of them be empty," Cade suggested. "That way, if we happen to find water, we can fill the empty canteens."

Baldwin nodded. "That's a good idea. All right, get saddled up, and we'll be on our way."

BALDWIN, Cade, Billy, and Amos had been out for the better part of an hour when they halted.

"I think it's time we spread out our hunting pattern a bit. Cade, you go south, Billy, you go west, and Amos, you go east. I'll stay here. If any of you see anything, don't try to engage; just get back here and report. And there's no need to go too far. Be back here within an hour, and we'll continue on together. If you aren't back within an hour, I will assume something has happened to you."

The three scouts nodded, then went out in their assigned directions.

About twenty minutes after Cade left, he smelled smoke. Dismounting, he tethered his horse, then moved ahead on foot. As the smell of smoke grew stronger, he became more cautious in his approach, finally finding some low-growing mesquite that offered him enough concealment for a closer examination.

There, below him, were four or five campfires, and in addition to the smoke he could also smell the aroma of cooking meat. There were no tipis, and no signs of women or children. This was clearly a war party, and Cade decided to get back to Baldwin to report what he had found.

Just as Cade turned, he saw an Indian approaching him. The man was armed with a war club which, at the moment, was raised above his head.

As soon as the Indian realized he had been seen, he brought the club down sharply. Cade rolled away just in time, and the club buried itself in the ground. As the Indian was trying to withdraw it, Cade put his left hand on the club, then sent his right fist into the Indian's jaw. The Indian lost contact with the club and rolled to his right. Cade stood up, and as the Indian, still on the ground, attempted to pull his knife from a sheath at his waist, Cade kicked him in the head. He saw blood and a couple of teeth flying from the Indian's mouth as he collapsed, unconscious from the blow.

Cade hurried back to his horse and, mounting, galloped back to rejoin Baldwin. The other two scouts were already back.

"We were about to give up on you," Billy teased.

"I found them, Lieutenant. The main body we've been looking for," Cade reported.

"How many are there?" Baldwin asked.

"I would guess as many as a hundred," Cade said. "I didn't stay to count them."

"All right, men, we've done our job, or, that is, Cade did our job for us. We need to—"

"Look out!" Chapman suddenly shouted, and looking around, Cade saw a dozen or more Indians riding toward them. Each was carrying a lever-action rifle, and they began firing, then jacked another round into the chamber and pulled the trigger again.

Baldwin and his scouts were outnumbered, and because the attacking Indians were armed with Winchester and Henry repeating rifles that had been issued to them by the agency, Baldwin and his scouts were also outgunned. The four men were all seasoned fighters, but the rifles they had with them, while good for long-distance shooting, were worthless for close-in fighting.

Fortunately, the four men were also armed with pistols, and ironically, the pistols gave Baldwin and his scouts an advantage over the Indians who, mounted with their long guns, were not able to get off aimed shots. Baldwin and his men returned deadly accurate fire, and of the original twelve Indians who'd attacked, only four were able to ride away.

One of the Indians had been de-horsed during the fighting, and as the others rode away, he stood up and yelled at them. If he was asking one of them to come back for him, he was wasting his breath, because no one returned.

"Well, it looks like all your friends have left you," Cade said.

The Indian turned. "Yes, they have," he said, speaking English.

"What the hell?" Amos said. "You got red hair. Damned if I ain't never seen me no red-headed Indian before."

"That's because I ain't no Indian. I'm a white man, 'n my name is Toby."

"Then, Toby, what the hell are you doin' with them savages?" Amos asked.

"I got took up by 'em when I was about five or six. Don't know for sure how old I was."

"Do you have a last name, Toby?" Lieutenant Baldwin asked.

"I had one, but I don't 'member what it is."

"Well, who are your parents?"

"Sasha Quiet Stream is my *nahkoeehe.* I have no *nehoeehe.*"

"I'm not talking about the Indians that raised you. I'm talking about your real parents, your white parents. What were their names?"

"Mom and Pop," Toby said.

"Mom and Pop? That's all you know?"

"Yeah."

"Lieutenant, we'd better get back to the general," Cade suggested. "The ones that got away will tell the others we're here, and they will for sure tell them there are only four of us."

"What about the white Indian here?" Amos asked.

"We'll take him back with us."

"How are we goin' to do that? He don't have a horse," Amos said.

"He can ride behind me," Billy offered.

"What if he shoves you off and steals your horse?"

"He won't try anything like that," Cade said.

"How do you know?"

Cade smiled and took his rope from where it hung on his horse. "We'll have a noose around his neck," Cade explained. "If he tries to run, we'll break his neck."

"I ain't a' goin' ta try 'n run away," Toby said.

Cade chuckled as he looped the rope around Toby's neck. "No, I wouldn't think so."

"THEY DEFINITELY KNOW we are here, General," Baldwin reported when the scouts returned to General Miles' base camp. "And they have us outnumbered and outgunned."

"Who is this?" General Miles asked, looking toward the young redheaded boy in Indian dress and paint.

"My name is Toby, 'n I want to thank you for saving me."

WITH THE GERMAN Wagon

"Somebody's comin'," Stephen called, coming back to the others to report his observation."

"Who is it, do you think?" Lydia asked.

"I don't know, just two men in a wagon."

"Stop the wagon, Lydia, and we'll wait for them," John said, but he raised his rifle as a precaution.

"I could use the time to walk around a bit," Lydia said. Stopping the wagon, she set the brake, then wrapped the reins around the brake handle. She had just climbed down from the wagon when the two men approached.

"Howdy," John called out.

"Well, hello," the driver of the wagon replied. "Who might you folks be?"

"We're the German family. This is my wife Lydia, my son Stephen, and my daughters, Rebecca, Catherine, Joanna, Sophia, Julia, and Addie." John indicated each one as he called their name.

"We're going to Colorado," Addie said.

"Colorado, are you? Well, you don't have far to go. We left Fort Wallace this morning, so you'll probably make it there tomorrow."

After visiting for a while, the two men bade them goodbye, then drove off toward the east.

"Is Fort Wallace in Colorado?" Sophia asked after their unexpected visitors had gone.

"No, it's still in Kansas, but I think it's right close to the line."

"Papa, that means we could be in Colorado in just a few more days. That means our long trip is over, doesn't it?"

"Well, not quite over," John replied. "It would be good to stop over for a day or two at the fort since it's been so long since we've had anybody to talk to."

"I'm really tired of this long trip," Julia complained.

"We all are, honey, but you just wait. It'll all be worth it," John told her. "Trust me, when we get there, you'll love Colorado so much, you'll wish we'd come a lot sooner."

10

THE CROWING ROOSTER ANNOUNCED THE DAWN, AND FROM HIS position on a blanket under the wagon, Stephen groaned.

"Ma, how about we have chicken soup today? I'll even clean and gut that rooster for you right after I kill it."

"No, Mama! Don't let Stephen kill my rooster!" Addie called down from her bed in the wagon.

"Your brother's just teasing you, Addie," Lydia said. "He isn't going to kill your rooster."

"I wonder, if I tie his beak shut, will that keep him quiet in the morning?" Stephen asked.

"No," Addie protested as she climbed down. "Bud wouldn't like that."

"Bud?"

"That's his name."

"Since when?"

"I named him Bud, but I kept it secret," Addie told them.

"It's not much of a secret. You just told everyone."

"Oh, I did, didn't I?" Addie put her hand over her mouth.

Stephen laughed, then walked over and hugged his little sister.

"All right, little one, I won't hurt Bud."

"Girls, get some wood gathered for the fire," Lydia directed.

Catherine and Joanna started gathering sticks, twigs, and whatever else they could find for the morning campfire. Sophia opened the chicken coop to scatter grain for the chickens.

As Stephen built the fire, John dug a hole in the dry creek bed until he hit water. Lydia and Rebecca began preparing breakfast.

Julia and Addie were running around, chasing one another.

"You girls stay close to the wagon, you hear me? Don't get out of sight," Lydia called.

When all the morning chores had been attended to and breakfast was eaten and the cooking utensils put away, John and Stephen hitched up the team of oxen and Lydia climbed into the driver's seat.

"Who's going to ride with me this morning?" she asked with a smile.

"Me!" Addie called. "I'll ride with you."

"Me too," Julia said.

Once the two girls had climbed up to the wagon seat, Lydia unwrapped the reins from the brake handle and released the brake.

"Heeh-ya!" she called to the ox team, and the two sturdy animals started up the gentle slope toward the trail.

NEARBY, and for the moment unseen by any of the German family, Medicine Water, Buffalo Calf Woman, and seventeen other Indians watched as the wagon started up the hill. One of them started forward, but Medicine Water held out his hand.

"Not yet," he ordered.

AS THE GERMAN family continued on their westward trek, the cattle, which had strayed about a hundred yards to the north, were being turned toward the wagon by Stephen and Catherine.

"It's a wonder they don't just run off," Catherine said.

"Where would they go? Cattle are herd animals. They would rather stay with us than run away."

Back at the wagon, with Lydia driving and Julia and Addie riding, Rebecca, Joanna, and Sophia were walking alongside, and John was riding in front.

"John," Lydia called. "There's something wrong with the wagon tongue."

John reached down to the harness of one of the oxen and stopped it, then dismounted and walked back to check.

"Ahh, a chain has come loose from the double tree," he said. "That'll only take a minute."

"I wonder why Pa stopped the wagon?" Catherine asked.

"It looks like something's wrong with the tongue," Stephen replied. "Catherine, will you take the cows back by yourself? I see an antelope. We can eat well for the next week if I can...oh, my God! Indians! Run to the wagon, Catherine. *Run!* Pa! Ma! Indians!" Stephen shouted at the top of his voice.

ON THE RIDGE, Medicine Water realized they had been seen.

"We go now!" he said, urging his horse forward. They covered the distance quickly, then, instead of charging right up to the wagon, Medicine Water led the Indians as they circled the wagon.

"Get back here. Hurry!" John shouted as Stephen and Catherine returned, breathing hard from their run.

Sophia saw her father lift his rifle to fire, but before he could pull the trigger, one of the Indians fired, and her father dropped the rifle as he fell face-down. That was when she saw blood from a wound in his back.

The Indian started toward him, and Sophia saw with shock that the Indian was carrying a hatchet. He brought it down sharply, plunging the blade into her father's head.

"No!" Lydia screamed, jumping from the wagon and running toward her fallen husband

"Mama, Mama, come back!"

"Oh, just let me go to Father! Let me go to Father!" Lydia screamed as she ran.

"John, John!" she cried, sinking to her knees beside him. Several Indians dashed up to her then, and all of them started beating her with their war clubs. She fell next to John, and one of the Indian gashed open her head with a hatchet. That was when Catherine saw that the Indian who had wielded the hatchet was a woman.

"Go away! Go away!" Rebecca shouted and, grabbing the axe from its place on the wagon, she stood there facing the Indians who came toward her. She swung the axe but missed, and before she was able to lift it for a second try, she was knocked down. As she lay on the ground, several of the Indians jumped off their horses and began pulling off her clothes until Rebecca was naked. One of the Indians spread her legs, dropped to his knees, lifted his breechclout, and began raping her.

"What is he doing?" Sophia asked.

"Don't look," Joanna said, turning Sophia's head away.

"But what is he doing to her?" Sophia asked again.

"Get off her, you son of a bitch! Get off her!" Stephen shouted, grabbing the Indian and physically jerking him away from Rebecca. For his effort, Stephen was shot by at least three of the nineteen Indians who had attacked the wagon.

Catherine ran over to the wagon to be with her other sisters. The five young girls were shocked beyond all sensibility by the carnage they were watching being inflicted on their family.

In the meantime, the Indians, who had satisfied themselves with Rebecca, now grabbed blankets from the wagon and, laying them over Rebecca's inert form, set them on fire. Any thought that she might already be dead was disproved when Rebecca called out in alarm. Screaming in pain, she tried to escape the burning bedclothes, but one of the Indians came over and hit her in the head with his hatchet and Rebecca grew quiet.

Catherine, Joanna, Sophia, Julia, and Addie stood by the wagon, shocked by what they had just seen and terrified as several of the Indians approached them.

"Stand in line," one of the Indians said, speaking English.

Sophia had seen this particular Indian giving orders to the others, so she assumed he was in charge.

"Stand in line," the Indian said again, and this time, he put his hands on their shoulders and physically placed them in position. Because Joanna was taller than Catherine, the Indians, thinking she was the oldest, made the mistake of putting her first in line. Now all five girls, Catherine, age seventeen, Joanna, age fifteen, Sophia, age twelve, Julie, age seven, and Addie, age five, waited to see what was going to happen. Addie was making little snuffling sounds and her bottom lip was trembling, but there were no audible sobs and no tears.

Several of the Indians came over to examine them, and after a moment or two, their conversation grew louder and more hostile, but the hostility was directed toward one another. The girls realized they were arguing among themselves. Finally, the argument was settled, and one of the Indians jerked the bonnets from the heads of the five terrified youngsters.

Joanna's long, beautiful hair was freed now, and it fell in cascades below her shoulders. Catherine and Joanna were pulled out of the line and taken a short distance away from the others.

"Here! What are you doing?" Catherine called out, realizing at that moment that she was now the head of the family. "Leave us alone!"

The Indians ran their hands through Catherine's hair, then through Joanna's hair. Again, they began talking among themselves and pointing at both Catherine and Joanna, although more frequently at Joanna. Sensing that something was about to happen to her, Joanna called, "Sophia, tell Drew I love—"

That was as far as she got before one of the Indians shot her in the forehead.

The Indians began their scalping then, starting with John, then Stephen, then Lydia. They didn't touch Rebecca, as her body was being consumed by flames. Two of them came over to Joanna's body. One of them grabbed her long blonde hair while the other began to scalp her, doing so carefully with a knife, rather than the brutal desecration the hatchets had dealt the others.

Returning to the wagon, the Indians began looting, taking what appealed to them and discarding the rest. One of them held up a blue vase and gave a shout of triumph, showing it off.

"No!" Julia shouted, running toward the Indian. "That's Mama's vase!"

With an angry swipe of his hand, the Indian knocked her down. Catherine and Sophia ran to her.

"Sophia, Addie is all alone," Catherine said. "Go to her. I'll take care of Julia."

Recognizing her big sister's authority now, Sophia did as she was told.

A moment later, Catherine returned with Julia, and the four girls stood there awaiting their fate.

With the Miles Expedition

"No coffee this morning, I'm afraid," Major Biddle announced as the soldiers were roused from their night's sleep.

"No coffee? 'N would the major be tellin' us how an army is supposed to go on the march without coffee?" one of the soldiers asked.

"Ha, Mick, most of the time you have more whiskey in your cup than coffee anyhow," another teased.

"We don't have enough water," Major Biddle explained. "We have to ration what we have until we find some."

"I know where there is water," Toby said. "I know where all water is."

A few minutes later, having been informed of their captive's claim, of knowing where there would be water, General Miles sent a couple of men out with Toby in search of water.

"ARE you sure there's water here?" Sergeant Caviness asked after the three men had gone several miles away from the camp. "We were through here a few days ago and we were lookin', but we didn't find no water."

"I think it's over there," Toby said. "I go look."

Sergeant Caviness and Private Lemon dismounted and watched as Toby, riding a cavalry horse, started toward the ridge he had pointed out. They waited for a few minutes for him to return with news of success or failure.

"Sarge, don't you think that boy ought to be back by now?" Lemon asked.

"Yeah, it seems so, don't it? Let's ride up to the top of that ridge and see what's going on."

When they crested the ridge a minute later, they saw no water. At first, they didn't see Toby either, but then Lemon pointed him out.

"Sarge, look. Ain't that him?"

Toby was at least a mile distant, riding away at a gallop.

"The son of a bitch is running away!" Sergeant Caviness said angrily.

"You think we should go after him?" Lemon asked.

Sergeant Caviness shook his head. "No. It's more 'n likely he's going back to join the Indians. If we chase him, we'll be ridin' right into a trap."

"Why would he do somethin' like that?" Lemon asked. "I mean, him bein' a white boy 'n all."

"He was raised by 'em," Sergeant Caviness replied. "Hell, he's more Indian than he is white by now."

"I hate havin' to go back 'n tell the others what that kid did, but most of all I hate sayin' we didn't find no water," Lemon said.

"Yeah, me too."

. . .

LATER THAT MORNING, Lieutenant Pope arrived with the howitzer and the two Gatling guns.

"Did you bring water?" General Miles asked.

"No, General," Pope replied. "I'd hoped you had water. We're on short rations now."

"We have to find water, or else we have to abandon the chase," Miles said. "Our situation is getting desperate. I've seen some of the men cutting gashes in their arms so they could moisten their lips with their own blood."

"General Miles, the boy is coming back!" one of the men called.

"Good, good! Perhaps he has found water after all!"

At first Cade, like the others, was encouraged by the sight of Toby, but there was something in his demeanor that gave them pause. Instead of coming on into the camp, Toby stopped, then turned in his saddle to look behind him.

"General, there's something wrong here," Cade said.

"What is it?" Miles asked.

"I don't know exactly, but why has he stopped like that? Why isn't he coming in?"

Toby stood in his stirrups and pointed to the bivouac of soldiers. He yelled something in Comanche, and suddenly several hundred Indians appeared over a distant ridge. Then, shouting at the top of their lungs, they began galloping toward the soldiers.

At first, none of the soldiers were in position, and many of them had their weapons stacked. They scrambled to get to them and take up defensive positions.

Cade realized that the soldiers' situation was not a good one. They were out in the open with nothing to provide cover, not even a depression in the earth. They were up against a superior number, and an enemy that was armed with repeating rifles versus their single-shot carbines.

The Indians' initial fusillade was fired from too far out, and the bullets whistled by harmlessly. There were, however, a lot of bullets, because the Indians had only to snap the lever down to jack another round into the chamber, ready to fire.

As the Indians drew closer, their fire became more accurate. Cade, like the other scouts and the buffalo hunters who had come with them from Adobe Walls, was armed with Big .50 rolling-block breach-loading weapons, but like many of the soldiers, only a few of the hunters had their rifles in hand. Cade did have his rifle, and he aimed at one of the galloping Indians and pulled the trigger. Even from where he stood, he could see the spray of blood erupt from the Indian's chest as he fell from his horse.

Then Cade heard something he had never heard before—the rapid fire of the Gatling guns. Both of them were firing now, and they were spitting out more bullets in a minute than the total number the Indians had used since they began their attack. Several of the Indians were unseated and their horses, their saddles empty, kept coming, many of them to be caught by the soldiers.

Joining the Gatling guns was the howitzer, and an exploding shell took down three more. The remaining Indians turned and retreated, leaving dead warriors and horses on the field behind them.

With the Captive German girls

As she sat astride a horse behind one of the Indian warriors, Sophia turned to look back toward the wagon. There, she could see the mutilated and scalped bodies of her family. She thought of her mother and her sister Joanna, both of whom would brush their long hair exactly one hundred strokes every night. Now both her mother's and Joanna's hair had been divided up among the warriors, and strands were attached to the bows or lances or tied to the ponies' halters. It was very easy to tell the difference because of the bright golden color of her sister's hair.

Sophia had never before been on a horse that was running so fast, and she was afraid she would fall off. As much as she hated the body contact, she wrapped her arms around the warrior in front of her.

They splashed through a creek of clear running water, and Catherine called, "Water! Please, let us have a drink of water!"

The Indians paid no attention to her and, thinking they didn't understand English, she began making scooping motions with her cupped hands, holding them to her mouth.

The Indians passed over the creek without stopping.

No more than half an hour later dark clouds appeared, and shortly thereafter, the sky was split by jagged streaks of lightning. Each flash was followed by a roar of thunder, then the rain came down in thick, heavy drops. Still the Indians didn't stop, and Sophia and her sisters held their faces up with their mouths open to catch what rain they could.

Although the thunder and lightning were frightening, the rain was a welcome relief from the heat. Before long, though, it was no longer welcome because they went from being very hot to being cold. The thunder and lightning passed, but the cold rain continued, and, their dresses soaked, the girls began to shiver.

After riding for some distance, they reached a village where there were women and other children. The four girls were taken from their horses, and although the rain had stopped, they were still wet and cold.

A couple of Indian women approached the four girls. They were carrying buffalo robes, and they passed them out to the girls.

"I am Little Squaw," one of the women said in English.

"What is to become of us?" Catherine asked, her lip quivering.

"Stay here now," Little Squaw replied.

"Are we going to be killed like Mama and Papa?" Julia asked.

Little Squaw shook her head.

"Is it because we are children?" Sophia asked.

"You will not be killed."

"Then why did they kill our brother and our sisters?"

"Stephen and Rebecca were not children," Catherine said. "I think they will not kill us." Catherine was doing what she could to allay the fears of her sisters, feeling obligated, as the oldest, to look after them as best she could.

The Indian who had led the attack came over to stare at each one of the sisters. Catherine had never seen anyone with as frightening a countenance as his.

"I am Medicine Water," he said. He pointed to Catherine. "Come. You belong to me now."

"I don't want to leave my sisters," Catherine protested.

Medicine Water slapped her, and Catherine cried out in pain and fear.

"You will come." He yanked her arm as he pulled her along behind him.

"Catherine!" Sophia shouted fearfully.

"It'll be all right," Catherine called back over her shoulder. "Look after the little ones, Sophia. I know it will be all right."

"I'm so scared," Julia said. "What is he going to do with Catherine?"

"I don't know," Sophia said, but even as she answered the question, she remembered what the Indians had done to Rebecca. And afterward, they had killed her.

A few minutes later, Little Squaw, the woman who had given them the buffalo robes, came to them.

"You and you," she said to Julia and Addie. "You come with me."

"What are you going to do with them?" Sophia asked.

"I will not hurt them," Little Squaw assured her.

Because Little Squaw had given them the robes earlier, Sophia felt she would not harm her younger sisters. And she knew, also, that under the circumstances, this was the best she could hope for.

CATHERINE HAD NOT SEEN Little Squaw come to claim Julia and Addie. She did try to look around, but every time she did, Medicine Water very roughly jerked her head away. He shoved her into one of the tipis, though "tipi" was not yet a word that Catherine knew. To her, it was just a tent made from some sort of animal hide.

"Take off clothes," Medicine Water demanded.

"What? No, that's all right. My dress will dry soon."

Medicine Water slapped her. "You are my squaw now."

"Your squaw?"

"Take off clothes," Medicine Water repeated, and although he didn't hit her again, he drew his hand back as if he would if she didn't comply.

Crying now, and with shaking hands, Catherine stripped out of her wet dress. A moment later, she was standing before him totally nude, and her embarrassment competed with her fear to be the dominant emotion.

"Down." He pointed to a buffalo robe.

Catherine knew what men and women sometimes did together, but seeing what had happened to Rebecca was the first time she had ever been a witness. That had been terrifying, even before her sister was killed.

Medicine Water forced Catherine down, then he stripped in front of her so that, within a moment, he too was naked.

With his foot, Medicine Water forced Catherine to spread her legs. Then he came down on her, and a second later, she felt excruciating pain.

With General Miles

CADE HAD BEEN the first to discover it. On one of the Indian ponies they had caught, there was a skin flask of some sort, and when he examined it, he discovered it was filled with water. The flask held at least three times as much water as any of the soldiers' canteens, and every Indian pony they had captured in the Indian attack—twenty-two in number—as well as nineteen more dead ponies had a full water flask.

There was enough water to fill every soldier's canteen, with water left over. General Miles rewarded his men by telling them they could drink as much as they wanted, then refill their canteens from the water pouches.

Cade, Billy, and Bat were given the task of counting the dead Indians for the official report the general would be making.

They had counted forty-four when Bat called to the others, "Cade, Billy, you'd better come over here. I think you should see this."

When Cade and Billy answered Bat's summons, he was looking down at one of the bodies. It was that of the young white boy who had identified himself as Toby. There were three bullet holes in his bare chest, the blood turning dark. His hair looked bright red in the sun, and he looked even younger in death than he had while he was alive.

"He couldn't have been more than fifteen or sixteen," Bat said. "It was a short life."

"As far as I'm concerned, he lived too long," Billy said. "We took him in, and the little son of a bitch betrayed us. The bastard led the others to us."

"Well, to be fair to him," Cade said, "this was the only life he knew, so he was doing what he thought was necessary."

"Yeah, well you've got a hell of lot more pity for the son of a bitch than I do," Billy said.

When they returned to the bivouac, they reported to General Miles.

"We counted fifty-two, General," Billy said. "And I'm damn sure they took some of their dead back with them."

"We lost six men," General Miles said. "On balance, we came out very well, although I hate the loss of any soldier."

"General, one of the dead we found was the boy Toby," Bat reported.

General Miles sighed and shook his head. "He didn't even know his parents' names. I fear we will never learn his story. What a tragic life he lived."

"Yeah, well, if you ask me, it's just as well that we don't know who his family is," Billy said. "There would be no joy in telling them we had located him, only to add that he died a traitor."

"Yes," General Miles agreed. "Some mysteries are better left unsolved."

With Mackenzie's Scouts

SHORTLY AFTER ESTABLISHING A CAMPSITE JUST SOUTH OF THE Colorado River, Jacob Harrison and a Tonkawa conducted a scout of the area. They had gone out less than two miles when Jacob discovered three converging Indian trails in the vicinity of the head of Pease River.

Jacob and the Tonk returned to the site where the D company had set up their camp.

"Well, from the look on your face, seems to me like you might have discovered somethin'," Sergeant Major Wilbur said as Jacob dismounted.

"I think I have," Jacob said.

"What do you say we go see the only other white man in this bivouac and ask him what he has to say about it?" Sergeant Major Wilbur suggested, a smile crossing his face.

The only other white man in the bivouac was Captain Beaumont, who was the commanding officer of D Company of the 10th Cavalry.

"Cap'n Beaumont," Sergeant Major Wilbur said as they approached him.

"I think Ranger Harrison may have found something you might want to hear about."

"What is it, Jacob?" Captain Beaumont said.

"I found what looked like three Indian trails, Captain. All three came together, then led off as one trail heading south," Jacob reported.

"To the Indian village, do you suppose?"

"It could be," Jacob agreed. "The Tonk thought that too."

"Great!" Captain Beaumont said. "As soon as Colonel Mackenzie and the regiment come up, we'll take a look."

When Mackenzie arrived later that day, Captain Beaumont sent for Jacob, and Jacob gave his report again.

"If you would like, Colonel, I can follow up on the trail and see where it leads," Jacob suggested.

"No, I think it might be better to do a reconnaissance in force," Mackenzie replied. "I'll take everyone out first thing tomorrow morning."

"Yes, sir."

"Colonel, have we heard anything from General Miles yet?" Captain Beaumont asked.

"No, I haven't heard anything from the *colonel*," Mackenzie answered, coming down rather pointedly on the word "colonel." "I expect we'll be getting a courier anytime now."

EARLY THE NEXT MORNING, before the reconnaissance in force got started, Sergeant Major Wilbur came to speak to Jacob.

"The colonel wants to see you, Ranger."

"All right."

"It's my thinkin' that you won't be gettin' no breakfast," Wilbur said. "So if you would like me to, I can round you up a biscuit 'n bacon."

Jacob smiled. "If you could come up with a cup of coffee to go with it, I'd be most appreciative."

Jacob found Colonel Mackenzie talking to Captain McLaughlin and Captain Beaumont.

"You wanted to see me, Colonel?" Jacob asked as he approached them.

"Yes, Harrison, I do. I'm going to send you out ahead of the rest of us. You are to be my eyes, and I mean eyes only. Do not, under any circumstances, engage the Indians. That is, of course, unless you are attacked and must defend yourself."

Jacob chuckled. "If I see Indians, there are bound to be quite a few of them. And believe me, Colonel, I have no intention of taking them on by myself."

Mackenzie nodded.

THE SOLDIERS WERE STILL at breakfast when Jacob rode out of the bivouac. With the reins wrapped around the saddle horn, Jacob was guiding the horse by applying pressure with his knees. Thanks to the sergeant major, he was holding a tin cup of coffee in one hand and a bacon and biscuit sandwich in the other.

Once he reached the three Indian trails he had come across the day before, he followed them until they converged. Then he followed the single trail to Sweetwater Creek, at which place it joined a very large trail that depicted the passage of a very substantial number of Indians.

Jacob hurried back to report to Mackenzie and the others, who had just broken camp.

"We've found the Indians, Colonel," Jacob said.

"You saw them?"

"No, but I sure as hell found their trail. And I don't mean just a few of them," Jacob said. "From the looks of things, I'd say there have to be four or five hundred of them."

"I wonder what they're doing this far out?" Mackenzie asked.

"Colonel Miles is also in the field," Captain McLaughlin said, being careful to refer to Miles by his actual rather than his brevet rank. "If you were to ask me, I'd say he and his men have probably pushed them down here."

"Yes, I would presume that you are right. Gentlemen, when we reach the trail, I want to follow it in three files. Major Biddle, you will be one mile to the east but proceeding in the same southerly direction. I ask that you not lose contact with us, but rather keep a constant exchange of couriers with me,"

"Yes, sir," Major Biddle replied.

"Captain Beaumont, you will be one mile to the west, and your orders are the same. Maintain a steady direction to the south and keep constantly in touch."

"Yes, sir," Captain Beaumont replied.

"I'll bring up the middle." Colonel Mackenzie flashed a big smile. "Gentlemen, let's pay a little visit to these Indians, shall we?"

With salutes, both officers returned to their respective commands, then took up the march.

With Miles

REFRESHED by the water they gleaned from their engagement with the Indians, General Miles proceeded to the Washita River, where they found an adequate supply of water for both the men and their stock.

By now the horses were pretty well exhausted, so General Miles made the decision to have a prolonged bivouac until the animals were sufficiently recruited. After they were encamped, Cade, Billy, and Lieutenant Baldwin were sitting in the shade of a cottonwood tree, eating hardtack and smoked buffalo. A soldier approached them and saluted Lieutenant Baldwin.

"What is it, Dorsey?" Baldwin asked, returning the salute.

"Sir, General Miles wants to see you."

"All right. Thank you."

"What do you think he wants?" Billy asked.

"Whatever it is, I'm guessing we won't be spending another night here," Baldwin said.

"By we, do you mean everyone? Or just us?" Billy asked.

Baldwin chuckled. "Gentlemen, I appreciate your opinion of my rank and authority, but I can guarantee you that if it is his intention to move everyone out, I would not be the first one he summoned. It means just us."

Cade laughed. "You know what I think? I think the lieutenant has made his point."

Lieutenant Baldwin took two more large bites of his buffalo, then set his mess skillet down and pointed. "That meat better be there when I get back, and I'm talking to you, Billy Dixon."

"Don't worry, I'll watch it for you," Billy promised.

"Ha! If that ain't settin' the fox to watch the henhouse," Amos Chapman teased.

When Lieutenant Baldwin approached the command tent, he found General Miles talking to Lieutenant Henely.

"Lieutenant Baldwin reporting as ordered, General," Baldwin said with a crisp salute.

"Frank, I don't know what the problem is with Camp Supply. I know from messages I've received that Captain Lyman was dispatched with a supply train some time ago," General Miles said. "He should have been here by now."

"You want me to find where it is now," Baldwin said. It wasn't a question, it was a statement.

"Yes. It is imperative we either find Lyman or get word to Colonel Lewis that we have to have replenishments, and soon."

"Very good, sir," Baldwin replied. "I'll get my scouts out immediately."

"No, I can't afford to have your whole scout out on patrol. I want this to be small—no more than six men. Frank, you choose your best men; that is, if you know who your best would be."

"That's easy, sir," Baldwin replied. "That would be Cade McCall,

Billy Dixon, and Amos Chapman. Normally, I would add Bat Masterson, but he's already on courier duty to Colonel Lewis, and I don't think he'll be returning to the field."

"Why not?" Miles asked.

"He said he's had enough of scouting, and after he gets to Camp Supply, he plans to hire on as one of the quartermaster's teamsters."

"What about Plummer?"

"If you recall, I strongly suggested that Plummer move on when the buffalo hunters from the Walls went to Camp Supply," Baldwin said. "And I will go out as well."

"No, I don't want you on this scout. Send those three, and you pick three of your best from your company, Austin. I'm sure they'll move past several war parties before they reach Supply."

WHEN BALDWIN RETURNED to the others, Billy Dixon and Amos Chapman were playing a game of "stretch." It was played by seeing how close they could throw a knife to each other's foot. If the knife stuck within a finger's width of the target he would have to open his legs by a foot. If the strike was farther than a finger's width, the thrower would have to spread his legs by a foot. It continued until one of the players could no longer stand. Both Billy and Amos had their legs stretched so far apart now that the end of the game was imminent.

"What did you find out?" Cade asked.

Baldwin looked at the three men. "I need six volunteers," he said as he picked up his skillet.

"What would we be a volunteerin' for?" Chapman asked.

"How many days have we been living on pilot bread?" Baldwin asked. "And soon we will be down to prairie chickens and rabbits, if there are any still alive in this drought-stricken desert. We've got to get a supply wagon in here, or it's over for this expedition."

The three men looked at one another.

"You can count on us," Cade said. "I suppose you want us to go with you to Camp Supply."

"That's where you'll be headed, but I'm afraid you'll be going alone. General Miles has asked Lieutenant Henely to send three of his troopers with you, but that's it. And needless to say, you'll be very short on rations."

Just then Lieutenant Henely and three men approached. "Gentlemen, Sergeant Woodhall and Private Harrington and Private Smith will be with you. They're good men, all three of them."

"There's no need to tell you, but I will anyway. Travel at night, sleep in any protected spot you can find during the day, and never be without a lookout. Like the general said, who knows how many war parties you will have to get past?" Lieutenant Baldwin said. "And men, I'm going to add Godspeed. I can't impress upon you enough—the success or failure of the Miles Expedition may depend on this one mission."

TWO DAYS LATER, just as the sun was rising, Cade, Billy, Amos, Woodhall, Harrington, and Smith neared a divide between the Washita River and Gageby Creek. Riding to the top of a little knoll, they found themselves almost face to face with a large band of Comanche warriors.

"Damn!" Billy said. "Boys, this doesn't look good."

The Indians saw the scouts as soon as the scouts saw them.

"We have to get out of here!" George Smith said, on the verge of panic.

"No, we're better off if we stand and fight," Cade said. "If we run, they can pick us off one at a time. At least this way, we'll be together."

"Dismount," Billy said. "Smith, hang on to the horses. If they get away, it'll be all over for us."

The Indians began firing at them and one of the bullets clipped Cade's arm, cutting a shallow groove. Cade returned the fire and killed the Indian who had shot him.

"Uhn!" Smith grunted as he fell to the ground. When he went

down, the horses bolted and ran.

"There go our mounts!" John Harrington shouted, although no announcement was necessary.

Cade was wearing a thin cotton shirt, slightly bloused, and he could feel more bullets popping through the loose fabric. Miraculously, except for the first superficial wound, none of them actually hit him.

The Indians kept up a heavy barrage, and it was obvious from their numbers that they could overrun the small group of defenders anytime they chose. Harrington gave voice to the observation.

"What the hell are they hanging back for?" he shouted.

"The sons of bitches are just playing with us, like a cat and a mouse," Chapman shouted back. It was necessary to shout in order to be heard over the incessant gunfire.

"We have to improve our position!" Cade yelled.

"Look, just ahead!" Billy said. "There's a buffalo wallow! If we can make it there, we might have a chance!"

"I'm hit, I'm hit!" Chapman called.

Looking toward him, Cade saw blood pumping out of the bullet hole just below Chapman's knee. His leg was soaked with blood.

"Come on," Cade said, going to him. "I'll take you with us!"

"You can't do it. I'm too big. Go with the others and leave me here."

"I'm not going to leave you." Cade turned his back to him. "Climb on, and I'll take you piggyback."

Billy, Woodhall, Harrington, and Cade started toward the buffalo wallow, which was about a hundred yards in front of them. Because Cade was burdened with Amos, he was considerably behind the others, but as soon as they made it to the wallow, the three turned and began shooting toward Cade and Amos. When Cade saw an Indian fall dead right beside him, he knew they were providing cover, and the accuracy of their shooting enabled him to make it to the wallow. Billy and John Harrington took Amos from Cade's back, and Cade fell to the ground, breathing heavily.

13

"WE NEED TO DIG OURSELVES IN AS BEST WE CAN," BILLY SAID AND, using the same knife he had been using in the game of stretch, he began digging.

The others began digging as well, and because the bottom of the wallow was loose sand, they were able to make good progress. As they dug, they threw up the sand around them until they managed to build a little wall that gave them more security and confidence.

By now, a few of the Indians, seeing that the white defenders were managing to improve their position, stopped their taunting and made efforts to close on them and finish them off.

"Let's dig in turns!" Cade suggested. "Billy, you and Amos hold off the Indians while Sergeant Woodhall, Harrington, and I dig."

Because of Amos's wound, he was not asked to dig, but he was able to fire at the Indians as the other four rotated jobs, so there were always three digging and two shooting.

"Come get us, you sorry, low-assed sons of bitches!" Amos shouted. "I'll cut your hearts out 'n—" Several of the Indians fired at Amos at the same time. The bullets hit very close to him, and because his mouth was open with his curses, it filled with dirt. Amos made a gagging sound.

Despite the precariousness of their situation, the other four men laughed.

Amos spat the dirt out. "You're crazy, you know that?" He spat again, then he laughed too. "Hell, we're all crazy."

"We all know these bastards may wind up getting us in the end," Cade said, "but I say we kill as many as we can now." Cade shot, and another Indian dropped. "And if we are killed, we'll look these sons of bitches up on the other side and kick their asses all the way to the devil."

"Sounds like a good plan to me," Harrington said, shooting and killing an Indian who was coming toward them.

"There's a couple of 'em going after Smitty," Woodhall called, speaking of Private Smith.

"He may be dead, but I don't intend to let the sons of bitches start hacking away on him," Billy said. He and Amos fired, and the two Indians who were trying to get to Smith were killed.

Cade, Billy, Chapman, Woodhall, and Harrington were in the middle of the wallow sitting back to back in a five-armed star, and in such a position, they had all approaches covered. In this defensive posture, they were able to keep any Indian from sneaking up on them, and because their ammunition was limited only to what they had with them, they were careful to get maximum effect with what they had, hitting an Indian almost every time they fired.

"Here comes three of 'em," Billy said, and looking toward Billy's coverage area, Cade saw three Indians galloping toward them with their lances raised. All three Indians were giving blood-curdling yells, but their yells were cut short when Cade, Billy, and Amos fired at almost the same time. The Indians were shot from their saddles, and their riderless horses galloped by.

The sun was blisteringly hot, and their canteens were still with the horses that had run away with the opening fusillade. Cade's tongue and lips were swollen with thirst, but he couldn't do anything but wait it out. Then, at about three o'clock in the after-noon, there was some relief as black clouds covered the sun. Soon after that, thunder and lightning started, presaging a rain that fell in torrents.

Water began to gather in the bottom of the wallow, and even though it was muddy, just as soon as it was deep enough to do so, all put their heads down, sucking up the water through extended lips. But the rain, gladly received at first, soon became unwelcome when what had been a very hot day turned cold with the rain and wind.

Despite the cold, on balance, the rain was a blessing. Not only did it provide them with much-needed water, but it also interrupted the attack. The Indians gathered just out of range, where they sat wrapped in their blankets and robes. Cade and the other four had neither blanket nor poncho. The five men were wearing nothing but thin shirts which were soaked through. That made the bitter cold even colder.

"Damn, I wish I had taken my coat off my saddle," Amos said, wrapping his arms around himself. By now, Amos and the others were shivering as if they were suffering from palsy.

"I miss my coat too," Billy said, "but what I miss more than the coat is what's in the pocket."

"I know what you're talking about," Cade said. "It's your mother's picture, isn't it? You've shown it to me before."

"Yes, my dad gave it to me just before he died."

"The water's getting deeper," Harrington said.

"Hell, we might drown before we get shot," Cade suggested, and the others laughed.

"By the way, how is everyone doing on ammo?" Billy asked.

"I'm all right for now," Amos replied. "But that ain't sayin' I'm not gonna run out."

"Somebody needs to get Smith's pistol and cartridge belt," Cade suggested.

"I'll go," Billy offered.

"Why? I'm the one who suggested it," Cade replied.

"You're also the one who brought in Amos. I'll go."

"All right. We'll keep you covered," Cade told him.

Cade, Amos, Woodhall, and Harrington watched as Billy splashed through the mud to Smith's body.

"Hey!" Billy called back. "Smith's not dead!"

"Damn, you mean we've left Smitty out there all this time?" Harrington asked.

"Trooper, it isn't as if we did it on purpose," Sergeant Woodhall said. "He hasn't moved a muscle since he fell. We thought he was dead. *You* thought he was dead."

"Yes, but now that we know, we can't just leave him there."

"One of you come out here and help me. I think the two of us could get him back," Billy called.

Without waiting for a second invitation, Cade climbed up from the wallow and hurried out to join Billy.

"George, we're sorry," Cade said. "We wouldn't have left you out here if we'd known you were still alive."

"That's all right," Smith said weakly.

They got Smith on his feet, and with Cade on one side and Billy on the other, started back to the wallow with him. But even as they were taking him back, Cade knew that the young soldier didn't have long to live. Smith had been shot through the left lung, the bullet going all the way through his body, and every time he took a breath, Cade could hear it whistling out through a hole alongside his left shoulder blade.

Moving as quickly as they could with Smith's feet dragging, they returned to the wallow with him.

"It's not going to do him all that good to let this muddy water get into his wound," Billy said. He was wearing a silk scarf around his neck and, removing it, he wadded it up and started poking it into the hole in Smith's back, the exit wound being considerably larger than the entry wound. When that was done, they lay him down in the two inches of water that had gathered.

"I'm sorry it's so cold, Smith," Cade said.

"I'm not cold," Smith replied.

"You're not cold?"

"I'm not cold," he repeated. Cade and Billy exchanged meaningful glances.

The men were cold and hungry, but there was nothing they could do about that. Then, just before nightfall, Cade got an idea.

"I know how we can keep ourselves out of the water tonight," he said.

"How?"

Cade smiled. "Tumbleweeds."

Tumbleweeds were all over, and for the next several minutes, Cade, Billy, Woodhall, and Harrington gathered rather large bundles of the ubiquitous disembodied plant. Most of the bundles were considerably larger than a bushel basket, so it didn't take very many to fill the bottom of the wallow. Once that was accomplished, they crushed them into a mattress. Their efforts had the desired effect of providing a somewhat dry cushion, making it more comfortable for them to lie down.

By the time it was totally dark, the rain had stopped, and the Indians were gone. Despite that, and despite the fact that they planned to sleep in shifts, nobody was able to sleep at all.

"Fellas," Smith said, "shoot me, please." He groaned in agony. "Somebody shoot me. I can't stand it anymore."

"Nobody's going to shoot you, Smitty, so you can just be quiet about it," Harrington said. "Besides, you owe me two dollars. Iffen I was to shoot you, how'd I ever get that two dollars back?" he added, trying to make a joke.

"Please, I beg you. Shoot me. *Shoot* me," Smith said again as he tried to lift his hand.

Smith's incessant pleading for someone to shoot him finally stopped at about ten o'clock that night when he fell asleep.

"I'm glad he's asleep," Chapman said. "He was really beginning to get on my nerves."

"You can't hold it against him, Amos. He has to be in terrible pain," Billy replied.

"Yes, well, my leg don't feel all that good either, and I ain't begging no one to shoot me," Amos said. "But I guess a bullet in the leg ain't like a bullet through your chest."

Although Smith was no longer begging to be shot, he wasn't quiet. His breathing came in gasping wheezes, then there were a couple of short gasps followed by silence.

"Check on him, Cade," Billy said.

Cade tried to find Smith's pulse and got nothing. There was no breathing, and no movement of any kind.

"He's dead."

"I'm glad his suffering's over," Harrington said. "But I'm even gladder none of us had to end it for him."

Now, with the clouds gone and the moon shining brightly, some of the discomfort, if not the danger, had passed.

"I wonder," Cade muttered.

"You wonder what?" Billy asked.

"A hundred, maybe a hundred and fifty years from now, this whole area might be a town, and right here in this wallow, kids might be playing. I wonder if anyone will realize then that on this very spot, six men were once engaged in a desperate life-and-death battle."

Billy laughed. "You know, Cade, sometimes you say the damndest things."

THE LONG NIGHT FINALLY PASSED, and though Cade had thought he didn't sleep any during the night, he was awakened by the warmth and the light of the morning sun.

"Hey, wake up," he said to the others. "It's morning."

"How about some coffee?" Billy asked.

"It's too late. I drank it while the rest of you were still sleeping."

"I'll bet you ate all the damn bacon, too," Billy teased.

"Fellas, one of us is goin' to have to go for help," Amos said.

"Yeah, you say that, seeing as it won't be you since you can't walk," Billy joked. "But you're right; someone does need to go, so I'll do it."

"No, you stay here," Cade said. "If you leave, it will weaken our position here. You're too good a shot."

"What do you mean, I'm too good a shot? You're just as good as I am," Billy said.

"Oh? Haven't you been telling everyone your shot was twenty yards longer than mine?" Cade asked with a smile.

"Well, that's true. All right, *you* go. But don't get your ass killed out there, Cade. The rest of us will be counting on you."

"I'll try my best not to get shot."

CADE LOOKED out of the wallow and, not seeing any Indians, slipped over the edge. Moving with the utmost caution, he began his mission to get help for his friends and himself. Within half a mile, he found the trail to Camp Supply and started following it. He hurried as quickly as he could, all the while keeping a lookout. Then he saw people moving ahead and took cover. The group continued toward him, and he saw with great relief that it was a group of soldiers.

Exposing himself, he fired into the air. The gunshot caused the approaching men to stop, and Cade fired again. This time two soldiers approached him, holding their carbines at the ready as they did so.

"Am I ever happy to see you!" Cade told them with a broad smile.

"Who are you, Mister?" one of the two soldiers asked.

"I'm Cade McCall. I'm a scout for General Miles. Our supplies are damn near exhausted, and the general sent us to find out where in the hell the supply wagons are. We were on our way to Camp Supply when we were jumped by a whole passel of Indians, and we've been fighting 'em off for two days. When we got a chance, I came for help."

"Yeah? Did you come for help, or did you run away? Why didn't the others come with you?" the corporal asked.

"One of the men is wounded and can't walk. Another was killed."

The corporal nodded. "All right, we'll take you to Major Price, but if you're lying about this, he'll have you thrown in the stockade."

Major Price was in command of the 8th Cavalry, and they were accompanying Captain Lyman's supply train that had been headed for General Miles' field headquarters. Price recognized Cade as soon as the two soldiers brought him to their commander.

"Mr. McCall," Price said. "Are you bringing a message from General Miles?"

"Yes, sir," Cade replied. "General Miles sent us to find the supply train. I guess I've found it, but that's not my problem now. Billy Dixon, George Smith, Amos Chapman, Sergeant Woodhall, Private Harrington, and I were attacked by a couple hundred Indians, George Smith died, and now those four are holed up in a buffalo wallow about a mile back. Chapman is wounded and can't walk."

"I'll bet it's the same damn bunch that had Captain Lyman under siege," Major Price said. "We managed to break it, and they may have happened onto you. I'll send some men out after them. You say Chapman is wounded?"

"Yes, sir."

"Then I'll send the Army surgeon too. You tell them where to go, but I'd like you to stay here and give me the details."

"All right," Cade agreed.

He gave directions to the soldiers and had just started telling Major Price about their encounter with the Indians when he noticed that the rescuers were going too far north. He fired into the air to get their attention and waved them in the right direction.

When Cade fired, the sound was within earshot of the wallow, and the men thought that more than likely, Cade had been killed by the Indians. As soon as the approaching troops were in range, one of the men shot at them, taking out one soldier's horse.

Seeing what the men were doing, Cade began running toward the wallow, yelling as loud as he could. When they saw Cade, the three able-bodied men stood up and began to cheer.

The Army surgeon examined Chapman's leg, then wrapped it in bandages.

"This will take care of you until some troops from General Miles' headquarters can rescue you."

"What do you mean, 'General Miles' headquarters?'" Billy asked. "After what we've been through, you're not taking us with you?"

"I'm sorry. Major Price says we can't be slowed down by taking you. General Miles has been too long without supplies as it is," the surgeon said.

"That doesn't make sense. We need to get back to Miles' headquarters, and you're going to Miles' headquarters, and yet you won't take us with you?"

"I can leave you some jerky and hardtack, but that's all we've got with us."

"What about ammunition?"

The soldier looked at the guns the men were carrying and, shaking his head, told them the bullets they had were the wrong caliber.

Cade and Billy headed to the train to see Major Price to plead their case, or at the very least, to have them take Amos Chapman with him.

"No, I can't do it," Price replied. "I'll notify General Miles of your plight, and I'm sure he'll send a detail out as soon as we get there."

"Will you at least leave some of your men with us?" Billy asked.

"I can't spare them," Price replied.

"Sir, I counted fifty-one soldiers, including you," Cade said. "And you've got eighteen wagons with two drivers apiece. Are you sure you can't leave us five or ten men?"

"No. What would we do if the train was attacked by Indians again?" Price asked.

Cade and Billy both laughed.

"I guess we'd be the wrong people to ask about that," Cade said.

WHEN PRICE and his men had moved on once again, the five men were alone in the wallow. Fortunately, no more Indians appeared for the rest of the day, and they prepared to face yet another night. At least there had been no more rain, so this night passed a bit more comfortably than the previous one, although the pain in Chapman's leg was becoming more intense.

And then they waited yet another day.

"You boys should go on," Chapman said. "Who knows when we will be attacked again, and I don't want to be the one that gets you killed."

"I won't leave you here," Cade promised

"And neither will I," Billy added.

"Me 'n Harrington won't go either," Woodhall added.

"That's plum foolish. You'd best save yourselves."

"That bastard Price said he'd get word to General Miles, and surely he'll do that," Cade said. "No, we'll all wait together."

They watched the sun set on yet another day of isolation, then, at about midnight, they heard the sound of a distant bugle.

"Listen!" Cade said. "Hear that?"

"Sounds like a bugle," Billy replied. "But what would they be doin' blowing a bugle in the middle of the night?"

"Maybe they're trying to signal us," Harrington offered.

"Let's fire three measured shots," Cade suggested.

"Not all of us. We're gettin' low on ammunition," Billy said.

Cade fired. *Bang...bang...bang.*

The sound of the bugle grew closer.

This time Billy fired three rounds.

A moment later, soldiers appeared out of the darkness.

"Here! We're over here!" Cade called, and the others joined in.

"Are we ever glad to see you!" Billy stated as the soldiers arrived. "That is, you are comin' to get us, aren't you?"

"We are," Captain Tupper said. "And man, oh man, did Major Price get an ass-chewin' from the general when he found out that bastard left you out here."

"Good," Billy said. "If any man deserved it, Major Price did. I hope I never run into him again, because I might have a hard time remembering he's an officer."

14

With the captives

AFTER BEING CAPTURED, CATHERINE, SOPHIA, JULIA, AND ADDIE German were in somewhat of a stupor, their condition brought on by both shock and weariness. The Indians kept going, moving faster and faster with few stops. By now, the girls were riding alone on horses provided by the Indians. They struggled to keep from falling off, and several times Addie lost her hold, falling to one side before managing to right herself. When Sophia got so tired she could hardly stay on the horse, they tied her feet together by running a rawhide cord under the belly of her horse.

Seven-year-old Julia was actually riding on one of the pack mules, and she slid off, falling under the mule's belly. The pack came off with her, which shielded her from the kicking mule. An Indian angrily snatched her up from the ground and put her on the mule again without bothering to secure the pack, almost guaranteeing that she would fall again.

The Indians moved steadily through the day and most of the night, eating only once a day, or sometimes not eating at all. They killed one of their own horses, not wanting to take the risk of hunting and killing a buffalo for fear of being discovered by the soldiers.

They ate the horsemeat raw, and although they offered some to the sisters, none of them would eat it despite how hungry they were. Then, on the third day, Medicine Water allowed Catherine to build a fire and cook some of the meat for her and her sisters. It was the first thing the girls had eaten since the breakfast their mother and older sister had cooked for them on the terrible morning they were attacked.

By the fourth day, having now come at least seventy-five miles south of the massacre, a few of the Indians left the main party. They looted and burned a store in the Kansas town of Pierceville, then stole several head of cattle from a nearby rancher.

A few days later, in the middle of the night, Medicine Water's band seemed to be confused. Several huddled together and held a whispered conversation. Of the four sisters, only Catherine was allowed to dismount, and she flung herself onto the ground, exhausted. Usually, Sophia, Julia, and Addie were tied to their mounts, but now they remained untied. Catherine felt great sympathy as she looked at them. How long could they remain upright without falling?

After the conference, about what Catherine had no idea, the Indians resumed traveling, doing so until daylight, when they rested. When they left again, Catherine was horrified to see that the sisters were to be separated. She and Sophia left with Medicine Water, while Julia and Addie were left behind with two of the younger warriors.

"Catherine, Sophia, don't leave us!" Julia called.

"Oh, please, please, let me go to my little sisters!" Catherine pleaded, and when she turned to do so, she was hit so hard that she fell off her horse. Getting up, she tried to run toward the little ones, but an Indian ran her down and swept her up, putting her back on her horse.

Catherine slowed her horse, hoping by doing so, it would allow her two younger sisters to join her, but one of the Indians lashed at the pony she was riding, causing it to gallop away. Catherine could hear Addie crying, and the sound rent her heart. A short while later, the two Indians who had been with the two younger sisters joined the main body, but Julia and Addie weren't with them.

"Where are Julia and Addie?" Sophia asked.

Catherine shook her head. "They're dead, I'm sure of it. The Indians didn't want to put up with them, so they killed them."

Sophia nodded. "Yes, I think you're right." She was quiet for a moment, then she spoke again. "You know what, Catherine? They're probably better off dead than we are alive."

Catherine thought of what Medicine Water had already done to her, and she was sure that she would have to suffer that degradation again and again unless he killed her. She was positive that same outrage would soon be visited upon Sophia.

"I think you're right, Sophia. At least they won't have to endure…" Catherine couldn't finish the sentence, and she fought to hold back sobs.

"Did it hurt?" Sophia asked.

"Did what hurt?"

"When he…uh…you know."

Catherine hadn't realized Sophia knew she had been raped. She didn't want to talk about it, but she felt obligated to say something to prepare Sophia for what she knew would be coming.

"It isn't pleasant at all, but it is bearable. Try to think about something else when it happens. Think about the good times we had when our family was all together."

With Julia and Addie

SHORTLY AFTER EVERYONE else had ridden off, the two younger warriors yanked Julia and Addie off their mules. Communicating with hand motions, they were instructed to follow, but the girls were too young, their legs were too short, and they were too tired to keep up. Julia and Addie watched the Indians ride away. Within a few minutes, the Indians who had stayed behind with them were out of sight and they were left all alone.

"What do we do now?" Addie asked.

Julia didn't have any idea what they should do now, but she was seven years old and Addie was only five, so she knew Addie would depend on her.

"Let's walk that way," Julia suggested, pointing in the direction they had seen their sisters going. "Maybe they've stopped somewhere and we can find them."

Julia had no real belief that they would find Catherine and Sophia. However, having some sort of idea of what to do, even if there was little hope of changing their situation, would make Addie feel better, Julia believed.

At about noon, they happened onto a depression in the ground that was filled with water. They saw a buffalo and a couple of yellow-eyed and very frightening-looking creatures drinking.

"Are those panthers?" Addie asked in a choked voice. "Papa told us about panthers, remember? They look like big dogs."

"I think they're wolves," Julia said. "We'd better get away from here."

The two girls left as quietly as they could. When they were out of sight, they began running, and they ran until both were out of breath. Then they collapsed, breathing as hard as they could.

After they had rested, the two began walking. No longer trying to follow the Indians, but just walking. Then Julia saw something that gave her hope.

"Addie, look!" she said, pointing to a trail. "Those are wagon tracks. Indians don't use wagons. If we follow them, maybe we'll find some white people."

Addie squeezed Julia's hand and smiled. "You are so smart," Addie said, showing the first bit of enthusiasm since the Indians had attacked their wagon and killed so many of their family.

"I'm awfully hungry," Addie said after they had walked for a while.

"I am too, Addie, but I don't know what..." Julia stopped and smiled. "I see food."

"You do? Where?"

"Right there, on that stem of grass," Julia said, pointing.

"I don't see anything."

"You don't see those grasshoppers?"

Addie wrinkled her nose. "You want to eat grasshoppers?"

"Why not? It says in the Bible that John ate locusts and honey, and a locust is a grasshopper."

"How do you know a locust is a grasshopper?"

"Don't you remember? Mr. Grant was our Sunday school teacher, and after he told the story about John eating locusts and honey, I asked him what a locust was. He said it was a grasshopper. Besides, Papa told us if we were hungry enough, we could eat bugs."

"I remember," Addie answered, "but you said you'd never eat a bug."

"I know, but this is different," Julia said as she caught a grasshopper and handed it to Addie.

"Oh, he's wiggling," Addie complained. "I don't want him wiggling around in my mouth."

"Then pull his head off," Julia suggested. "I'm going to pull his legs off too."

Julia killed the 'hopper, then stripped off its legs and popped it into her mouth. She chewed, then made a face.

"What does it taste like?"

"It's good. It tastes like popcorn." Julia lied because she was afraid if she told the truth, Addie wouldn't even try to eat it.

Addie popped it in her mouth and began chewing. "Oh, how could Papa and the man in the Bible eat these things?"

"Maybe they taste better with honey," Julia suggested, and Addie laughed.

"I don't want any more unless we find some honey," Addie said.

"Wait, I've got an idea." Julia caught another grasshopper, killed and stripped it, then popped it in her mouth. This time, instead of chewing, she swallowed it whole.

"Just swallow it," she said. "If you don't chew it, it won't taste as bad, and it'll be food for your stomach."

Addie did as Julia suggested, and as her sister had said, there was very little taste to have to deal with. They ate several grasshoppers that way until their terrible hunger, if not satisfied, was at least assuaged.

After eating, the two girls, dragging the shawl and worn blanket they had kept with them, followed the wagon tracks over a hill, then down to a swift-flowing stream. Here was water, and both girls fell on their stomachs and began drinking the clear, cool water.

"Oh!" Addie said when she had drunk her fill. "That tasted better than lemonade!"

"It *was* good, wasn't it?" Julia agreed. "Come on, we must be going."

"Why? Why don't we stay here? There's water and wagon tracks. Maybe if we stay here, the wagon will come back, or at least another one will come."

"It might be a month or two months before another wagon comes this way," Julia said. "But we can stay here for the rest of the day and night."

"Oh, look!" Addie said, pointing to some vegetation. "Green grass! Why can't we eat grass? Cows and horses eat grass, and Mama used to grow lettuce for us. I think it would be the same thing."

"Yes!" Julia said, happily, and for the next several minutes, the girls ate grass from blade to root. When they lay down to rest, it was the first time since leaving the wagon that they weren't hungry.

"I wish Catherine and Sophia were here," Addie said.

"So do I."

"Do you think they're all right?"

"I think so," Julia said. "If the Indians wanted to kill us, they would have kilt us the same time when they kilt mama and papa."

"And Stephen and Rebecca, and Joanna," Addie said.

As the two girls lay there on the blanket, a wolf appeared not more than ten feet in front of them. The animal's piercing eyes glared as it circled them a few times.

Terrified, the girls lay as quietly and as still as they could, taking short, shallow breaths. Then, thankfully, the animal trotted down to the creek, drank some water, and left.

Julia and Addie remained where they were for a long time, but as it began to grow dark, they gathered leaves and made a bed for themselves, using the blanket as a cover. During the night, more wolves and other prowling animals came for water from the stream.

"I'm scared," Addie whispered.

"Let's move our bed into the trees," Julia suggested. Once again, they gathered leaves to make a bed, this time back in the trees, away from the main path. They quickly learned that there were more animals around them in their new location than there had been before.

"What are we going to do?" For the first time, Addie began to cry.

"It looks like they're all coming to get water," Julia said. "We'll move our bed back into the bushes again, but this time, we'll make it farther from the water."

This time when they gathered leaves, they put their bed a lot farther from the stream. All during the night, they could hear the prowling animals, but they could tell the animals were farther away. Finally, out of sheer exhaustion, they fell asleep huddled in one another's arms.

With Catherine and Sophia

BECAUSE MANY OF the Indians could speak some English, Catherine and Sophia learned the names of their captors. The one who had led the raid on the German family wagon was Medicine Water, and his squaw was Buffalo Calf Woman. Although some of the younger Indian women could be considered attractive, Buffalo Calf Woman, who was quite large—larger even than many of the men—was an exceptionally ugly woman.

She was also very cruel.

"You eat now," she ordered, giving Catherine and Sophia raw meat, though whether the meat was beef, buffalo, or horse, the girls didn't know.

"We can't eat it," Catherine told her.

"Why no eat?"

"The meat is raw. We can't eat raw meat." Catherine pointed to a flaming campfire. "Let me cook it; then we can eat."

Buffalo Calf woman picked up a flaming brand, and Catherine thought she was asking a question about cooking.

"Yes, yes," Catherine agreed. "Cook for us."

"I no cook for you!" Buffalo Calf Woman said, and she threw the burning brand at the two girls. When the burning piece of wood hit the ground in front of them, it shattered, and burning embers popped onto both Catherine and Sophia.

Frightened, Catherine and Sophia embraced each other.

"If you no eat, you starve," Buffalo Calf Woman said, and she turned and stomped out of the lodge.

For a long moment after the woman had left, the two girls held each other.

"We'll survive this as long as we have one another," Sophia said. "Poor little Julia and Addie. How I wonder where they are."

"It's no use wondering," Catherine said. "In our hearts, we both know what happened to them."

"I know, but every night I pray to God that they are safe somewhere."

15

WHEN CADE, BILLY, AND AMOS REJOINED THE MILES EXPEDITION, THE surgeon took one look at Amos' leg and made a clucking sound as he shook his head.

"That's going to require surgery," Dr. Powell said.

"We'll send him to Camp Supply in the ambulance," General Miles said.

Dr. Powell shook his head. "We can't do that. Gangrene has already set in, and by the time we could get him there, he'd be dead. I'm going to have to take that leg now."

"Huh-uh. No," Amos said. "You ain't takin' that leg, Doc."

"I don't have any choice, Mr. Chapman. You're either going to lose that leg, or you'll lose your life."

"I'd rather die than lose my leg," Amos replied.

"You don't mean that, Amos," Cade said. "How many men do we know who lost a limb during the war? And how many of 'em can work as hard as they did when they were whole? Isn't that right, Doc?"

"It is," the surgeon said. "I've taken off quite a few limbs in my day, and not a single man said he'd rather be dead when it was all over."

"All right, but if I'm gonna let you do this, I'm gonna have to be awful drunk before you start."

"You'll be better than drunk," Dr. Powell said. "You'll be knocked out with laudanum. You won't feel a thing."

"Doc, are you sure you want to amputate his leg out here in the field like this?" General Miles asked.

"General, you were in the war, just as I was," Dr. Powell replied. "Surely you must have walked by a surgeon's tent at least once after a battle.

"Yes, I remember Fredericksburg," General Miles said. "Outside the surgeon's tent, at the foot of a tree, I noticed a pile of amputated feet, legs, arms, and hands. Why, there was enough to fill a wagon."

"And that was just on the Union side, and after one battle," Dr. Powell said. "I guarantee you the outlook was just as glum on the Rebel side. Trust me, General, I've done many an amputation in situations more primitive than this."

Despite the situation, Amos couldn't help but get off a macabre joke. "Seems to me, Doc, that the general ain't ought to be the one you should be askin' to trust you. I'm the one that's losin' the leg here."

The others laughed at the black humor.

"It'll take me a few minutes to get everything set up for you," Dr. Powell said, "so if there's anything you'd like to do before the surgery, now's the time to get it done."

"I'd like a drink," Amos said, and before Dr. Powell could reply, Amos held up his hand. "And I mean a real drink of whiskey, not that laudanum you're a' talking about."

"We're in the field, Mr. Chapman. Do you have any idea where you might come by a bottle of whiskey?" Dr. Powell asked.

"Sergeant Gibson," Billy suggested.

"What makes you think Sergeant Gibson would have a bottle?" Lieutenant Baldwin asked.

"How do you think Gibson manages to stay drunk all the time?" Billy asked.

"I've never seen Sergeant Gibson drunk."

Cade, Billy, and Amos laughed at the same time.

"What's so funny about that?"

"Lieutenant, you've never seen Rodney Gibson sober," Billy said.

When the whiskey bottle was produced a few minutes later, Chapman took several swallows, then handed the bottle back to Sergeant Gibson.

"Thanks, Gib."

"Yes, sir. Well, I just happened to have a bottle with me. Meant to leave it back in the barracks, but just forgot, is all."

"Here," Dr. Powell said, holding out a small vial of laudanum. "Drink this."

Amos tossed it down, then wiped his mouth with the back of his hand. "All right, Doc, start sawing away."

ALTHOUGH GENERAL MILES kept the bulk of his troops in bivouac, he sent Lieutenant Baldwin and his scouts, accompanied by Lieutenant Henely and forty troopers, to try to locate the Indians who had taken part in the Buffalo Wallow fight. Leaving just before dawn the next morning, they took the trail back to where the fight had taken place.

One of the first things they noticed after reaching the site of the battle was that the bodies of the dead Indians were gone. Cade checked the grave where they had buried Private Smith. His grave had not been disturbed, although the hastily constructed cross with which they had marked a fake gravesite had been destroyed and the "grave" dug up. Cade smiled as he realized the decoy had served its purpose.

"I'M GOIN' to get me one of them peg legs," Amos told Cade and Billy when they came back to the Miles encampment. "Only it ain't goin' to be one o' them wood ones. No sir, this here 'n is goin' to be made out of iron, so when I kick somebody's ass with it, they're goin' to damn well know they's been kicked."

"Hmm, I've heard about that all my life, and I've often wondered how it would work," Cade said.

"How what would work? What are you talking about?" Billy asked.

119

"Why, I'm talking about a one-legged man in an ass-kicking contest," Cade said, eliciting laughter from the others, and especially from Amos.

"Mr. McCall, Lieutenant Baldwin wants to see you," one of the soldiers in Henely's command said. "You'll find 'im in the command tent, talkin' to General Miles."

"Thank you, Schuler."

"Mr. McCall," General Miles said, greeting Cade when he showed up in response to the summons. "I have a dispatch for Colonel Mackenzie, and Lieutenant Baldwin has volunteered your services. Are you willing to do that for me?"

"Yes, sir. I'll be glad to do it."

"Also, if you don't mind, I'd like for you to stay with him for a while. Perhaps as much as a month," General Miles said. "The colonel may not be that pleased to have a pair of my eyes and ears in his camp, but I have overall command. I need to have a trusted account of his disciplinary methods."

"Sir, I'm not sure what you are asking of me."

Lieutenant Baldwin spoke up. "What the general is asking is for you to spy on Colonel Mackenzie. Reports are that Colonel Mackenzie has some rather arcane means of discipline."

Cade raised his eyebrows, still not knowing exactly what the two officers meant.

"It has been reported that Mackenzie allows his officers to string up enlisted men by their thumbs," General Miles said. "In my opinion, this is conduct unbecoming of an officer. If an Indian did that to a soldier, he'd be tried and put in prison."

"How soon do you want me to leave?"

"How about now?"

"Now it is."

16

With Catherine and Sophia

"Little Squaw, do you know where our little sisters are?" Catherine asked.

"They are gone," Little Squaw said as tears rolled down her cheeks. "Little Squaw is very sad that they are gone."

Buffalo Calf Woman, who overheard the exchange, said something to Little Squaw, but she spoke in Cheyenne, so the girls didn't understand what she was saying. However, the tone of her voice indicated she was taunting Little Squaw, and when she used her fingers to denote tears coming from her eyes, they were sure of it.

Little Squaw made no reply to the taunts, and finally, mercifully, Buffalo Calf Woman left the tipi.

"Did Buffalo Calf Woman talk mean to you?" Sophia asked.

"Yes," Little Squaw replied. Then she pointed to the raw meat. "You no eat?"

"It is not cooked," Catherine said. "We can't eat meat if it isn't cooked."

"I will cook," Little Squaw said. Finding a flat rock, she sat it right at the edge of glowing red coals. Then, with another rock, she pounded the meat to tenderize it and spread it out on the hot rock. Within minutes, the lodge was filled with the aroma of cooking meat.

"Oh, thank you," Catherine said. "That smells delicious!"

As Catherine and Sophia sat next to the fire, watching the meat brown, their stomachs growled with hunger and anticipation. Then Little Squaw lifted the meat from the cooking stone, cut it into two pieces, and handed the portions to Catherine and Sophia.

"No!" Buffalo Calf woman shouted, pushing her way into the lodge. She grabbed the piece of meat from Sophia and threw it in the dirt. Then, grabbing the other piece from Catherine, she began eating it, laughing loudly as she left the tipi.

Catherine began to cry then. So far, she had held her tears back, feeling like she needed to be strong for Sophia, but she had been through too much. First the killing of her parents, of Stephen, Rebecca, and Joanna, the long, tiring ride, going hungry, not knowing what had happened to her younger sisters, being raped repeatedly, and now this brutal attack from as evil a woman as Catherine had ever seen.

It was all too much for her.

"Don't cry, Catherine," Sophia said, "I'll clean the piece of meat up and we can share."

Sophia came over to embrace and comfort her older sister, and Catherine felt both ashamed of her own weakness and love for and pride in her young sister.

Then, as the two girls stood there, arm in arm, Little Squaw retrieved the piece of meat and carefully cleaned it off. Cutting it, she gave half to Catherine and the other half to Sophia. After that, she sliced off another piece of meat and began cooking it.

"Thank you, Little Squaw," Catherine said. "It is good to have a friend."

During the night, Catherine had a dream, although the dream was so vivid that she was certain it was real. She felt a warm and loving presence near her, then she was kissed on the cheek. After that, someone spoke to her in words that were soft but very distinct.

"Catherine, do the very best you can."

"Mama!" Catherine said, recognizing her sweet mother. She held out her arms to go to her, but her mother disappeared.

Catherine woke up then and saw the inside walls of the lodge gleaming in the golden light of the low-burning fire. Sophia was lying next to her on the buffalo robe, breathing softly in her sleep.

At first, Catherine was bitterly disappointed that what she had experienced had only been a dream, but then the disappointment faded, to be replaced by the joy of having seen her mother, and heard her comforting words. Catherine was convinced it was more than a dream; she truly believed that somehow her mother had actually come to see her.

Catherine put her arm about Sophia then and drew her close.

"Mama," Sophia said quietly.

Was Sophia having the same dream? Why not? If Mama had come to see her, why wouldn't she have come to see Sophia as well?

"Yes, sweetheart, it's Mama," Catherine said.

With Colonel Mackenzie

"ARE YOU A BUFFALO HUNTER?" The question was asked of Cade by a black man in uniform.

Cade smiled. "No, I'm not a buffalo hunter. Are you a buffalo soldier?"

Now it was the soldier's time to smile. "Yes, I am. Who are you?"

"My name is Cade McCall. I'm a scout and courier for General Miles, and I've come with a dispatch for Colonel Mackenzie."

The buffalo soldier turned and, cupping his hands around his mouth, gave a shout.

"A courier from Colonel Miles!"

"Let him pass," a disembodied voice replied.

After following the path pointed out by the sentry who had challenged him, Cade saw a very busy bivouac with several tents, at least half a dozen wagons, a few hundred horses in a temporary corral, and several campfires around which soldiers were gathered. He was met by a black soldier with the stripes of a sergeant major on his sleeves.

"You're the courier?"

"Yes."

"You aren't in the Army?"

"No, I'm Cade McCall. I'm a scout with Lieutenant Baldwin, but right now I'm serving as General Miles' courier."

"All right, Mr. McCall, come with me."

Cade followed the sergeant major through the encampment until they reached the largest tent in the entire bivouac. The guidon posted in front of the tent marked it as the regimental headquarters.

The sergeant major stepped in first, then came back out a moment later. "Colonel Mackenzie will see you now."

Cade nodded his thanks and went into the tent. The inside resembled a room more than a field tent. There were a table and chairs, a cot, and two kerosene lanterns mounted on poles. There was even a small carpet on the ground.

"Colonel Mackenzie, my name is Cade McCall. I'm a scout for General Miles, and—"

"You are a scout for whom?"

"General Miles, sir."

"I know of no General Miles. I am, however, aware of a Colonel Miles."

"Yes, sir, that would be the same. It's just that he was brevetted a general during the war, so I was paying him the courtesy."

"I was also brevetted a general, Mr. McCall, and yet you just addressed me as 'colonel.'"

"Yes, sir, I suppose I did. I'm sorry, I didn't realize—"

Colonel Mackenzie dismissed Cade's apology with a wave of his hand.

"Never mind, it's a petty thing. What's the dispatch?"

Cade handed over the leather case he was carrying.

Mackenzie opened the satchel, took out a brown envelope, and began to read. "It appears that our condescending field commander is once more at odds with the Department of the Missouri," Mackenzie said. "As a scout, I suppose you know General Pope has cut off supplies to Miles after the Lyman train fiasco."

Cade clinched his teeth to keep from saying anything he would later regret. "Sir, I do know General Pope has ordered that we get our supplies using our own men and wagons."

"And now he wants the *colonel* to haul his ashes out of the fire." Mackenzie laughed. "Well, Mr. McCall, you can tell your *colonel* that we in the Department of Texas have no trouble receiving our replenishments, and if they are delayed, we forage for our needs. But we don't intend to send one cracker to Miles. Good day."

"Uh, sir?" Cade stuttered. "Were there any other written orders from General Miles?" This time Cade purposefully used the word "general."

Mackenzie reexamined the satchel, then withdrew a folded piece of paper and began to read. Looking up, he stared at Cade for a long moment.

"What the hell did you do to piss off Miles? He wants you to stay with my command for a while."

"Yes, sir, he did mention that."

"You say you're a scout?"

"Yes, sir."

Colonel Mackenzie called through the opening of his tent, 'Sergeant Major Wilbur, is our Ranger scout close?"

"Yes, sir."

"Ask him to come see me."

When Cade looked toward the tent opening, he gasped in recognition.

"Jacob!"

"Cade? I thought you were in Tennessee."

"I came back."

"So you two gentlemen know each other?" Mackenzie asked, responding to the reactions of the two men upon seeing one another.

"Yes, sir. Friends and former business partners," Jacob said. "Harrison and McCall Freighting Company."

"Well, Mr. Harrison, your friend has *volunteered* to serve with us as a scout. Do you think you'll be able to work with him?"

"Yes, sir. I would love to have Cade with me. That is, Cade, if you..."

"Of course," Cade said slapping Jacob on the back. "But who's the—"

Jacob interrupted Cade before he could finish the sentence. "Colonel Mackenzie is the boss, and we never forget it."

Mackenzie laughed. "Don't ever let anybody forget that, Harrison." The colonel waved his hand to dismiss the two friends.

"I NOTICED that Colonel Mackenzie asked for the Ranger scout. Are you still a Texas Ranger?" Cade asked after they left the tent.

"I am."

"Then what are you doing here?"

"I'm in the Texas Frontier Battalion, and when Colonel Mackenzie put out the word he was looking for scouts, I persuaded Major Jones to let me join up with him."

"You like being with Mackenzie?" Cade asked.

"I do. There's nobody like him. He pushes and pushes his troops almost to the point of exhaustion, but there isn't a one of them who wouldn't go to the river for the colonel," Jacob said. "They all know he doesn't ask the lowliest private to do something he wouldn't do himself."

"That's interesting," Cade said.

17

With Julia and Addie

JULIA AND ADDIE HAD BEEN WANDERING ON THEIR OWN FOR AT LEAST three weeks, living off locusts, wild plums, hackberries, wild onions, and the roots of grass stems. Then they hit upon what they thought was a bonanza when they stumbled upon a former Army bivouac site that was near water. Here, they found bits of grain left from where the horses had been fed, a piece of cooked meat, a piece of cheese that was covered with ants, and several morsels of hardtack.

Even though their father had always told them never to camp at the same site for two nights in a row since he thought wild animals would retrace their steps if they had been unsuccessful in finding food, the girls remained at the bivouac site for three days, believing someone might return. When all the scraps were gone and no one had come, they started walking again, hoping to find someone somewhere who could help them.

Late in the day, every day, the girls would look for a place to spend the night. They searched for a spot that would keep them safe from the wolves and, if possible, protect them from the fall night winds that each successive night seemed to be getting colder. They found such a place in a depression in the side of a hill.

"Addie, you stay here," Julia ordered. "Don't go anywhere since you might get lost. I'm going to look for food."

"If you find something, bring it back so we can share it."

"I will," Julia assured her. "Remember, we promised we'd share anything we find."

"Come back before it gets dark," Addie said. "I don't want to be here by myself."

"Don't worry," Julia said as she hugged her sister. "I'll be back before it gets dark."

Addie watched her sister walk away, then pulled the blanket around her and curled up in the hole to wait. She thought about Catherine and Sophia. How she wished they were still together.

But what if the Indians had killed Catherine and Sophia the way they killed Rebecca and Joanna?

As she lay there, all curled up in the hole in the side of the hill, she saw several ants scurrying around something. She remembered that when they were in the place they had camped before, when they had seen a lot of ants together like that, it generally meant that they had found something to eat. She scraped away the dirt where the ants were and found a dirt-encrusted cracker! The soldiers must have come through this way, and one of them had dropped a cracker.

Scraping the cracker clean as best she could, Addie ate it without regard to the dirt that still clung to it. She thought it was the best thing she had ever tasted.

"Oh!" she said aloud. It wasn't until then that she realized what she had done. Addie had just violated the promise she and Julia had made to one another. She had eaten the cracker so quickly that she hadn't even stopped to think, and she began to cry in remorse over her transgression.

About half an hour later, Julia returned.

"See, I told you I'd be back before it got dark. I didn't find anything to eat, but I did keep my promise."

Addie began to cry again.

"Don't cry, Addie. We'll find something tomorrow. I know we will."

"That's...that's not why I'm crying," Addie sobbed.

"Then what's wrong?"

"Oh, Julia, I'm sorry. I didn't mean to, but I ate it. I just ate it before I remembered the promise."

"You ate what?"

"The cracker," Addie said. "I was just so hungry that I ate it without thinking. I'm sorry. I'm really sorry."

"You promised!" Julia said angrily. "We promised to share!"

"I'm sorry!" Addie said again, crying even more loudly.

Now both girls were crying, but after a few moments, Julia's anger subsided and she reached out to embrace her sister.

"I'm not mad at you," Julia said. "I know you didn't do it on purpose."

The two frail little bodies laid down then, embracing to keep warm until they finally cried themselves to sleep.

With Colonel Mackenzie in Bivouac

ABOUT THIRTY INDIANS appeared within a thousand yards of Mackenzie's encampment and tried to get the soldiers to pursue them.

"Colonel, they're right out there, just baiting us," Major Anderson said. "Why don't we go after them?"

"You said it yourself, Major. They're baiting us," Colonel Mackenzie said. "They want us to come after them so they can lead us into a trap."

"All right sir, if you say so. But I hate to just let 'em get away."

"They're not going to get away. It's just that I don't intend to fight the battle they have planned for us. I'd much rather fight a battle *we* plan."

"And what is our plan?" Major Anderson asked.

"First thing, I want to make sure they don't stampede our horses. Order the men to bed down in a circle and put the horses in the middle. Even put a double hobble on them," Mackenzie said. "I expect they may try to sneak in during the night to get them."

"Yes, sir," Major Anderson replied.

That night, the soldiers slept fully dressed in what they called "sleeping parties" of from twelve to fifteen men each. They formed a ring around the horses, with every third man remaining awake. The full moon was exceptionally bright, giving the sentries a very good view of the perimeter for some distance.

Colonel Mackenzie's warning proved to be accurate, since just after midnight, an estimated two hundred and fifty Indians, using feeder canyons, approached to within a hundred and fifty yards of the bivouac before making their charge. They struck right in front of D Troop, and Sergeant Major Wilbur gave the alarm.

As it turned out, the alarm wasn't needed since the warriors came in yelling, dragging buffalo hides, and in general making as much noise as they could. It was their intention to stampede the horses and leave the cavalry afoot, but the troopers were awake and waiting for them.

"Hold your fire, men," Captain Beaumont ordered. "Hold your fire until I give the word."

The soldiers, lying in the dark, waited for the order. Not until the Indians had come within thirty yards did he shout, "Now shoot the sons of bitches!"

Because the Indians had thought most of the soldiers were asleep, it wasn't until the soldiers opened fire that they even noticed them. Many of the marauders were killed in the opening barrage.

Realizing they wouldn't be able to stampede the horses, those Indians who had survived the initial attack retreated and joined the others who were waiting some distance away.

Many of the Indians could speak English, and they began yelling insults at the soldiers, hoping to draw them out.

"White eyes! Why do you not come to fight? Are you afraid of the Comanche?"

"White eyes are cowards!"

"Come fight us!"

"Our eyes ain't white, 'n neither are we!" Sergeant Major Wilbur shouted.

"Buffalo?" one of the Indians called.

"That's right, we're buffalo soldiers, 'n if you want us, come get us."

The taunting from the Indians stopped soon after that, but the shooting continued. However, it was long-range shooting, and except for the Indians who had been killed in the initial contact, the Indians suffered no additional casualties.

As dawn approached, the shooting became more intense, and though there were no casualties among the troopers, four of the cavalry horses were killed.

Mackenzie ordered two companies to saddle up and be ready to give pursuit. Both Cade and Jacob volunteered to go with them, and Mackenzie gave his permission.

"We can't let them stay where they are. They want our horses, and if they can't steal them, they'll shoot 'em," Mackenzie said. "I want you to drive the bastards away, but under no circumstances are you to follow them for more than two miles. Is that clear?"

LIEUTENANT BOEHM LED the troopers in pursuit and the men rode at a gallop, exchanging fire with the Indians, although since all the shooting was done from the saddles of galloping horses, only one Indian was unseated. The Indians were on swifter ponies, so the distance between them never narrowed. At the end of two miles, the Indians still had a lead of over a hundred and fifty yards.

"Bugler, sound *Recall!*" Lieutenant Boehm ordered, and at the bugler's call, the attacking troopers came to a halt.

"Ain't we goin' no farther after 'em, Lieutenant?" one of the soldiers asked. "Hell, we ain't kilt but one of 'em since we bin chasin' 'em."

"Our orders were to go no farther than two miles, and by my calculations, we've come that far. Column about!"

In a column of twos, the troopers swung around and headed back toward Mackenzie's encampment.

"Lieutenant, might I suggest Cade and I ride in the rear so we can make certain they don't come after us?" Jacob suggested.

"That sounds like a good idea to me, Ranger."

As the column started back, Cade and Jacob rode behind, keeping at least a hundred yards of separation. That gave them enough room to have ample warning time if the Indians did turn around and start after them, but the Indians made no such move. Within half an hour, all were safely back within the encampment.

"Sir, we pursued the hostiles for two miles, as ordered," Lieutenant Boehm reported. "They are out of our area, and I am pleased to report we had no casualties."

18

Over the next two weeks, Colonel Mackenzie sent out reconnaissance in force missions of never less than two companies in an attempt to locate the Indians. Although they encountered wandering bands of Indians during these protracted searches, they were never able to locate the main village of the hostiles. Their patrols were not without action, though, because the original operational plan drawn up by General Sheridan had envisioned that five separate expeditions would drive the Indians to a central location. This plan was meeting with success, as General Miles, Colonel Davidson, Colonel Buell and Major Price were all engaging the Indians, driving them farther and farther south, where they would be met by Colonel Mackenzie's forces as they moved north.

While out on a scout near the Freshwater Fork, Cade and Jacob came into visual contact with a group of hostiles.

"How many are there?" Cade asked.

Jacob took out his binoculars and began counting. "I see twenty."

"Make that twenty-two. There are a couple more over there," Cade pointed out.

"Twenty-five. I see three I missed. It looks like they're making camp."

"I wish they were on the move," Cade said. "Then we could follow them, and they might lead us to the main village."

"That'd help," Jacob added.

"Maybe we could force them to move," Cade suggested.

"Cade, you're not suggesting the two of us can do that, are you?"

"No, but Captain Beaumont can."

"ALL RIGHT, MEN, TO HORSE!" Captain Beaumont ordered after Cade and Jacob returned with their report.

As they were approaching the location where the Indians had been spotted, there was a gunshot from somewhere within the ranks.

"Troop, halt!" Captain Beaumont called, holding up his hand. He turned in his saddle to look back along the formation. "Who fired that shot?" he demanded.

"I did it, Cap'n," one of the privates said sheepishly.

"What were you shooting at?"

"I warn't shootin' at nothin', Cap'n. My carbine just went off, is what happened."

The troop continued on, but Cade was certain that because of the errant shot, the Indians would be gone. That concern was realized; when they reached the place where the Indians had been camped, they were no longer there.

"It's coming on night time," Captain Beaumont said. "We won't be able to track them in the dark, so we might as well set up for the night."

DURING THEIR SUPPER OF BACON, biscuits, and gravy, Jacob and Cade sat off by themselves. Jacob asked Cade about Dodge City.

"Truth to tell, I don't know a lot more about it than you do because I didn't stay there too long after I got back from Tennessee."

"Did you bring the half-breed back with you?"

Cade smiled. "No, I left Stone with my brother. He's a happy little kid, for all he's been through."

"And Jeter and Magnolia?"

"Still in Dodge City. Jeter's running The Red House, and Magnolia's raising children. Chantal and Bella are almost four, and the little one, Mary Lilajean, is a handful."

"They're good people," Jacob said. "I miss Dodge City."

"Would you ever think about going back?"

Jacob thought about Cade's question for a moment.

"I don't think so. I sort of like being a Texas Ranger." He laughed. "You seem to be following me around, Cade. When you're tired of scouting for the Army, you should come down and join up."

"I'll keep that in mind, but right now, I don't exactly know what I'll do next."

Just after nine o'clock, about two dozen Comanches came rushing into the camp of the bivouacking soldiers, catching them before the nighttime watches had been ordered. The Indians shouted and fired their weapons as they attempted to stampede the horses. There was total confusion among the soldiers as they tried to restrain their horses while taking potshots in the darkness. Finally, the Indians withdrew.

Not one trooper had been wounded during the night-time raid, and as far as they could determine, they had not hit a single Indian. But when calm was restored and they were able to take inventory, they discovered that more than half their horses had been run off.

"The half of you who still have your horses, mount up," Captain Beaumont said. "If we don't find them, it'll be a long walk back for some of you."

With Catherine and Sophia

CATHERINE AND SOPHIA had been captives for at least a month. During that time, Catherine had set about learning Cheyenne. She thought that if she could understand what the Indians were saying, it might give her some advantage. A boy who was somewhat younger than she likewise wanted to learn English, hence Mucclebee became Catherine's tutor, as well as her student.

Mucclebee and Little Squaw did what they could to relieve some of the harsh treatment that was visited on the two girls. While all Indian women did the majority of the work done in the camps—tanning hides, sewing clothes, packing and unpacking mules and horses, putting up and taking down lodges, gathering wood, and preparing food—they seemed to do these chores willingly while their man sat by. He was allowed and expected to beat his wife, or wives, depending upon how many he could afford.

It was in this environment that Catherine and Sophia labored. The chores they were assigned seemed to be exaggerated to emphasize how superior an Indian woman was to the two petite white girls. When they were made to saddle a mule, they were given the most unruly one, ensuring that the mule would kick the girl, causing everyone who watched to laugh uproariously.

Likewise, when they were told to carry water from the creek, the buckets Catherine and Sophia were given were half again as large as the usual ones. It was under these circumstances that Little Squaw and Mucclebee would step in to help them.

Buffalo Calf Woman, the person who had driven the hatchet into Lydia German's head, seemed to get the most pleasure out of torturing the girls. On one occasion, Catherine asked Little Squaw why Buffalo Calf Woman was so mean to her and her sister when she seemed so caring for her own young children.

"It is because of Sand Creek," Little Squaw explained.

"Sand Creek?"

"You do not know Sand Creek?"

Catherine shook her head. "I do not."

"It was a peaceful village of Cheyenne and Arapaho. Then one day, an evil soldier chief led many soldiers to that place. The chief of the Indians was Black Kettle, and he put up the soldiers' flag of stripes and stars and the white flag to show he would not fight. He told his people, do not fight.

"His people did not fight, but the evil soldier chief did not care. He had his soldiers begin to shoot, and soon, many squaws and many children die. They say five hundred die that day."

"Oh, my!" Catherine said, shocked by the information. "I didn't know that."

"All our people know story," Little Squaw told her.

"And this is why Buffalo Calf Woman is so mean? Because she has heard this story too?"

"Buffalo Calf Woman was there. Her husband, her baby, her mother, her father, her three sisters, all killed. Buffalo Calf Woman was stuck with long knife the soldiers carry. She close her eyes to make them think she dead. Now, she has much hate for white people."

"I can understand her anger, but I was not at Sand Creek, and my sister was not there. My mother was not there, but Buffalo Calf Woman killed my mother with a hatchet."

"It does not matter who was there or who was not there," Little Squaw said. She put her hand over her chest. "There is much anger in Buffalo Calf Woman's heart, and her anger is for all white people."

"Although I do not think that is right, I can understand the anger in her heart," Catherine said. "I too have anger in my heart, but I do not hate you or Mucclebee. You are both kind to me."

Little Squaw smiled and handed Catherine a piece of dried meat she had in her pouch.

"Here, you eat."

THAT NIGHT, Catherine bore in silence yet another sexual assault, this time from a man she had never seen before. She considered such attacks a rape of her soul as well as her body. When finally the man was satisfied, she laid on the pallet and cried bitterly. Between her sobs, she prayed aloud, thanking God that so far she had not conceived a child.

THE NEXT MORNING, Sophia had gone down to the creek to get water when the one she knew as Bear Shield came to her with another Indian. Bear Shield was both her guardian and her master.

"This is Wolf Robe," Bear Shield said. "Now you go to him."

It really didn't make any difference to Sophia who owned her, because except for Little Squaw and Mucclebee, one Indian was pretty much like any other. What did matter to her, though, was that she realized belonging to Wolf Robe meant she would be leaving this village. Even though she and Catherine did not see each other every day, they knew they were not far apart. Now she would be separated from Catherine. Would she ever see her sister again?

Sophia started to cry, but Wolf Robe slapped her.

"Do not cry," Wolf Robe ordered. "If you cry, I will beat you."

Sophia couldn't stop the tears from sliding down her cheeks, but she was able to stop sobbing. Wolf Robe tied her to a pony, then led her out of the village. She looked back over her shoulder at the tipi where she had last seen Catherine. She wanted to call out, but she was afraid.

"LITTLE SQUAW, do you know where my sister is?" Catherine asked when she hadn't seen Sophia for several days.

"Sophia has been taken," Little Squaw told her.

"Taken where?"

"Taken," Little Squaw said, unable to provide more information.

Catherine returned to the tipi and laid on the pallet, weeping. The last of her family was gone. It was as if her world had come to an end.

"Come!" Buffalo Calf Woman said a few minutes later. "You work."

"Where's my sister?" Catherine asked, refusing to move

Buffalo Calf Woman kicked Catherine as she yanked her to her feet. "You work."

Ironically, shortly after Catherine began doing her assigned task, gathering firewood, the work became therapeutic. The mundane repetition allowed her to clear her mind, causing her to stop grieving over the taking of Sophia.

19

CADE AND JACOB WERE RIDING ABOUT A QUARTER OF A MILE AHEAD OF
Captain Beaumont's troops when Cade saw something that got his
attention.

"Jacob, come take a look," he said.

When Jacob responded to the invitation, Cade pointed to the
ground just ahead of them. What he had found was a horse trail
heading south.

"Damn, that has to be more than a hundred horses, or maybe even
more than that," Jacob said. "I wonder how old this trail is?"

Cade dismounted, then walked over to examine a few of the
deposits left by the ponies.

"From the look of these droppings, I'd say no more than two or
three days."

"You think we can get Beaumont to see where it leads?" Jacob
asked.

"Why not? Isn't this what Mackenzie expects us to do? Find the
main village?"

"That's our job all right, but let's think about this a minute,"
Jacob said. "Beaumont has less than fifty men in this troop, and by
your own estimate, these tracks are from at least a hundred horses.

If they're headed for the main village, they could be joining anywhere from five hundred to a thousand warriors." Jacob shook his head. "You aren't going to get Beaumont to risk his men like that."

When they returned to Captain Beaumont with the report on what they had found, Jacob's observation proved true. Beaumont refused to commit his troops to follow the trail Cade had discovered.

"Mr. McCall, look at our horses. They're in such poor condition it's hard to get them to move, let alone if I have to put us in a position where we might have to fight. We've got to find a place with better forage and water where these animals can be recruited," Captain Beaumont said. "Otherwise, we're just courting disaster."

Cade wanted to argue with Beaumont, but he knew the captain was right. If they followed the path the Indians had taken, they could very well wind up riding into an ambush. And he knew that with the condition of the horses, it would be impossible to outrun the Indians should they be attacked.

It was with disappointment that Cade and the others headed back to meet Mackenzie.

A WEEK LATER, with their horses somewhat refreshed, Captain Beaumont's troop returned to Colonel Mackenzie's encampment, and it was from there Cade and Jacob went out on another scout.

"It looks like they turned off here," Cade said, examining the trail they had been following.

"I'll be damned. They're headed for the Palo Duro," Jacob replied.

"Let's go see what we can find."

"There's something odd about this trail," Jacob said as he dismounted. "There probably aren't more than fifteen horses, but what's strange is, they're not making any effort to cover their tracks."

"Pretty sure of themselves, I'd say, and you know what that means, don't you?"

"It means they're planning on joining a much larger group."

Cade smiled. "Jacob, I think we may be about to find the motherlode."

Dismounting, Cade and Jacob approached the rim of Palo Duro Canyon on foot. Then, to make certain they would not be seen against the skyline, they lay down and slithered to the edge.

"Damn, Cade, look at that," Jacob said, his voice reflecting his awe. "That's like seeing St. Louis in tipis."

Eight hundred feet below on the floor of the canyon, the two men could see hundreds of lodges.

"We have to tell Mackenzie about this," Jacob said, backing away from the edge.

Not until they were far enough away to be sure they couldn't be seen did the two men stand up. Then, as they started walking back, Cade saw something, and he stuck out his hand to stop Jacob from going any farther.

"What is it?" Jacob asked his voice barely above a whisper.

"We're about to have company."

Both men drew their pistols and held them down by their sides as they continued along the path toward where they had left their horses.

Suddenly four warriors leaped into the path before them. Two of the warriors had lances, and two of them had raised hatchets. With blood-curdling yells, the four Indians attacked.

Cade and Jacob raised their pistols and shot, each of them firing two times. Four shots were all it took.

"Think anybody down below heard those shots?" Jacob asked as he held the still-smoking pistol at the ready.

"It doesn't matter whether they heard them or not. We're far enough away that I doubt they'll investigate." Cade nodded toward the four dead Indians. "I'm pretty sure these were their lookouts."

"Not one of 'em has a gun," Jacob said, glancing at the bodies. "You have to admire these bastards. There aren't many cowards among them."

"Let's find a place to put these bodies in case somebody misses them," Cade said.

"With all the gullies around here, that shouldn't be too hard to do."

They left the canyon and rode back to Mackenzie's bivouac. It was very late in the afternoon when they returned, and the first thing they saw were ten wagons that had not been there when they left.

"Looks like Lieutenant Lawton got through with the supply train," Jacob said. "That's good. It means we'll eat a little better tonight than we have for the last month of Sundays."

"And the best thing is, the horses will have corn."

"DID you find any Indians this time out?" Sergeant Major Wilbur asked when Cade and Jacob dismounted after returning.

"We didn't just find Indians, we found all of them," Jacob replied with a big smile.

"I'll bet the colonel will be pleased to hear that," Wilbur said. "Give me your horses; I'll take care of 'em while you give him your report. Then come on back here, and I'll have your supper ready for you. We got more coffee today, so you can have as much as you want."

"Sergeant Major, I don't care what your troopers say about you. I think you're a good man," Jacob said with a chuckle as he and Cade surrendered the reins of their mounts to him and then headed to Mackenzie's headquarters to give their report.

"Wonderful news, simply wonderful!" Mackenzie said. "And now, with what our trains brought up, we'll be able to bring the harshest of punishments to the hostiles. Gentlemen, get some rest, for tomorrow we attack."

As he had promised, Sergeant Wilbur had supper for the Cade and Jacob when they returned. Tonight it was beef cooked with potatoes and onions. In addition, there was cornbread, and of course, coffee. They also enjoyed a peach cobbler made from canned peaches.

"I'll say this," Sergeant Wilbur said as he downed his own supper with the two scouts. "If I take my last breath tomorrow, at least I'll meet my Maker with a full stomach."

There was generally a feeling of happy anticipation among all the troopers who were with Mackenzie, and not just the black soldiers, because now Mackenzie had his entire regiment assembled. They realized they were about to do battle and they were looking forward to the prospect, not only because they felt like this might conclude their long days in the field, but also there was a sense of excitement.

"I plan to kill me about five of 'em," Trooper Jackson said.

"You goin' to kill five of 'em, huh, Jackson?" one of the other troopers teased. "What if one o' them five kills you instead 'n takes your scalp?"

Jackson reached up to clutch a bit of hair between his thumb and forefinger. "Now, why would they want a short, curly scalp like this when they can take some white boy's long yeller hair?"

The others, including Cade and Jacob, laughed.

THE SUN WAS JUST BEGINNING to send out a few faint streaks over the eastern horizon when Mackenzie's command, consisting of five companies of infantry and eight companies of cavalry, arrived at the precipice of the Palo Duro Canyon. Seven of the companies were with the 4th Cavalry, while one, D Troop, was with the 10th.

"McCall, Harrison, go take a look and see if you can determine whether or not our approach has been compromised," Mackenzie ordered.

"With the colonel's permission, sir, I would like to go with them," Wilbur said.

"Very well, Sergeant Major, you may go," Mackenzie said. "By the way, we'll have a cold camp this morning. I don't want the Indians to by chance smell the smoke or the coffee."

"Yes, sir."

Handing the reins of their horses to the man who would be serving as their handler, Cade, Jacob, and Wilbur walked the three hundred yards up to the rim on the canyon, then laid down to look over the edge.

"Holy shit, look at all of 'em," Wilbur said of the hundreds of lodges that were spread out along Palo Duro Creek, which ran through the floor of the canyon. "There must be a thousand tipis," Wilbur exaggerated.

"They don't suspect a thing," Jacob said.

"That's because they haven't discovered the four we killed," Cade replied.

"Yeah, it was a good thing we pulled them off the trail and hid them in the gullies," Jacob agreed.

"We need to get back to the colonel," Cade said after he had backed away from the rim of the canyon.

"THEN BY DAMN, we've got them!" Mackenzie said after the report. He made a fist of his bad hand and slammed it into the palm of the good one. "Sergeant Major, return to your troop. Major Pierce, get the men prepared for the assault. Mr. Harrison and Mr. McCall, you'll both be with me."

"Very well, sir."

NOW THE ENTIRE expedition proceeded to the rim of the canyon and looked down. Most of the men had never seen anything as large as the Palo Duro Canyon, and it was an awesome sight. Millions of years of erosion had created a canyon that at this point was eight hundred feet deep and six miles across. It was an ideal place for the Indians, providing a ready supply of cottonwood, cedar, wild cherry, mesquite, and hackberry trees to use for firewood, lodge poles, and arrows. Also available was a stream that meandered along the floor of the canyon, supplying fresh water that was constantly fed by the springs in the canyon walls.

"Well, now the question is, how do we get down there?" Major Price asked.

"That is a good question," Colonel Mackenzie replied.

"Colonel, on the way up here, we saw a trail going down into the canyon," Cade said. "It was about a mile back."

"How wide is this trail?"

"Narrow. Very narrow," Cade replied. "I think we can get down it, but only if we go single-file. And we won't be able to ride, but we can lead our horses down."

"Too dangerous," Major Pierce said, shaking his head. "We'll have to find another way."

"There is no other way, Major," Jacob said.

"And we'll likely not have another opportunity to find this many Indians congregated in one place," Colonel Mackenzie added. "If we go down very quietly, it won't take that long to put a company on the ground. That company will have to provide security for the rest of us as we come down. Lieutenant Thompson, take all your scouts down. Ranger Harrison and Mr. McCall will lead you. You'll need some troopers with you as well."

"Yes, sir," Thompson replied without hesitation.

"Captain Beaumont, you'll take D Troop, and Boehm, you'll take E Troop. As soon as you reach the canyon floor, deploy your troops in a defensive position so the rest of us can come down."

"Yes, sir," Beaumont and Boehm replied in unison.

THE TRIP down the trail was very difficult. It was more like climbing down than walking down, and the men stumbled, slipped, and slid, all the while leading their horses. Often the man behind would have to grab the tail of the horse in front to keep the horse from overtaking the man in front.

They were about two-thirds of the way down when they were startled by an Indian who was standing lookout on an overhanging rock. The Indian began to yell and wave a red blanket, hoping to get the attention of the villagers.

Without waiting for orders to do so, Cade raised his rifle and fired. The fifty-caliber round took the back of the Indian's head off, and he dropped instantly. The sound of the shot came rolling back in an echo from the opposite wall.

"Damn, they're going to have to have heard that," one of the other scouts said.

For an entire moment, the procession down the narrow trail stopped as everyone waited anxiously to see if either the lookout's warning or the sound of the shot had alerted anyone in the village. When there was no reaction from below, the detail continued their descent.

After an hour of stumbling, sliding, cursing, finding things to hold onto, and coaxing the horses, the scouts, Troop D, and Troop E were on the ground. Quickly, they formed a defensive perimeter in order to provide sufficient cover for the rest of the men to come down.

In the village, an old warrior had risen early and was relieving himself by a mesquite tree when he was startled to see several soldiers on the canyon floor. He fired two warning shots, then rushed back into his lodge.

Cade was certain that if his earlier shot had not roused the village, these two shots would but still, there was no general reaction.

"Damn, you know they heard that," Captain Beaumont said. "Why the hell hasn't anyone come out?"

"Maybe they just think this place is impenetrable," Jacob said as he looked around at the steep canyon walls. "Would any officer but Colonel Mackenzie have the nerve to bring his whole command down into this hellhole?"

20

As the number of soldiers on the ground increased, more Indians saw them, and the alarm spread quickly. With the alarm came panic, and the Indians began to scatter. All the women and children fled, many galloping up the valley on horseback, while others sought safety by scrambling up to hide in the crevices of the northwest wall.

Most of the warriors had grabbed their weapons and run to the same wall, where they took up defensive positions among the boulders and cedar trees. The other warriors made an effort to save their horses by trying to drive them away before the soldiers got there.

The troopers mounted their horses and, arranging themselves in a battle formation, charged. But when they arrived and galloped through the Indian encampment, they discovered that it was abandoned.

The people were gone, but the village wasn't empty. The ground was littered with blankets, clothing, cooking utensils, buffalo robes, shields, bows, arrows, even rifles and ammunition. These were the things they had to have in order to function in their nomadic life. It was obvious that the village had been caught by absolute surprise, and what had just happened was a disorganized rout rather than an orderly retreat.

Some of the Indians had made an attempt to pack their belongings on their animals but had abandoned the effort to flee with the others. As a result, many of these horses were now running about wildly with the loosely tied bundles, having slipped, now hanging below the horses' bellies. Other horses, which had been tied to the trees or tethered to the ground, pulled at the ropes in panic.

"Round up those horses!" Captain Beaumont shouted, and the men of D Troop started after them. Seeing the onslaught of soldiers bearing down upon them, the Indians who were trying to protect the horse herd abandoned their efforts and fled. As they galloped away, one Indian turned to fire at the soldiers, and Captain Beaumont's horse went down.

When they saw that one of the soldiers was down, the Indians stopped running. Several of them gathered to take advantage of the situation, and they began firing at Beaumont as he was trying to extricate himself from under his horse.

"Cap'n Beaumont!" Wilbur shouted, and he galloped into the storm of fire toward his commanding officer.

"No, Sergeant Major!" Captain Beaumont shouted. "Stay back. *Stay back!*"

The bullets continued to rain down on the fallen officer as he tried, without success, to free his trapped leg. Several bullets hit the horse, and more of them kicked up dirt around him.

When Sergeant Major Wilbur arrived, he dismounted and, hurrying toward Beaumont, went to the side of the horse that was most exposed to enemy fire.

"Get out of here now, Sergeant Major! That's an order!" Captain Beaumont shouted.

Wilbur grinned. "Well, sir, I reckon you're just goin' to have to court-martial me, 'cause I ain't obeyin' that order."

Sticking his carbine under the dead horse, Wilbur used it as a lever to try to relieve enough pressure on Captain Beaumont's leg for him to get it free.

"Can you pull it out now, sir?"

"Not yet," Beaumont replied, his voice strained by the effort.

"Let me see if I can help!" Cade said, running up to the two men at that moment.

"You're crazy," Beaumont said. "Both of you are crazy!"

Cade's Big 50 was longer than Wilbur's carbine, and because of that, he was able to provide more leverage.

"Sergeant, when I ease the pressure, see if you can pull his leg out," Cade said, lifting up on the end of his rifle to open up a small wedge.

With both Captain Beaumont and Wilbur straining at the leg, they were finally able to pull it free.

"It's out!" Wilbur called, but his happy shout was abruptly halted by a solid *thock*. The source of the sound quickly became obvious when blood erupted from the back of Sergeant Major Wilbur's head. He fell forward, his body lying across the dead horse.

"Sergeant Major!" Captain Beaumont shouted in concern.

Three of the Indians, believing that now they had the soldiers trapped, charged toward them. Captain Beaumont had been disarmed by the fall and Sergeant Wilbur was dead, which left Cade as one against the three.

But even as Cade was drawing his pistol, he heard a shot from behind him, and one of the Indians went down. Beaumont grabbed Wilbur's carbine and took down a second Indian, while Cade killed the third.

Looking around to see where his help had come from, Cade saw that Jacob had dismounted and was looking at Sergeant Wilbur.

"Wilbur?" he asked.

"Yes," Cade replied.

"I will put this man in for the Medal of Honor," Captain Beaumont said.

Beaumont took Wilbur's mount, and despite his injured leg, led his men in the roundup of the Indian herd.

When they returned to the village, Mackenzie was there, having ordered a thorough search of all the lodges. By now the warriors who had escaped the initial charge on the village had regrouped on the rim of the canyon. They were shooting down at the soldiers, and Mackenzie quickly realized that his position was untenable. He ordered a withdrawal to the streambed, where they were able to establish a defensive position.

"H Company!" Captain Gunther shouted. "Let's clear the hostiles out of there."

Several of his men stood to respond to his call, but Colonel Mackenzie intervened. "Hold up on that! Captain Gunther, I appreciate the courage of you and your men, but if you do that, not one of you will live to reach the rim."

"How are we ever going to get out of here?" one of the men asked, his voice reflecting his fear.

"Don't worry, trooper. I got you men in here, and I'll get you out," Mackenzie replied.

After a spirited exchange of fire, the Indians quit shooting.

"Why do you think they quit?" Lieutenant Boehm asked.

"I don't think they had much choice," Cade said. "They couldn't have taken much with them, as fast as they had to leave. More than likely they're out of ammunition."

"So you think they are just up there watching us with empty guns?" Captain Beaumont asked.

"I don't think they're up there at all," Cade replied.

"Mr. McCall, would you be willing to put that theory to a test?" Colonel Mackenzie asked.

"You want me to go up and see if they're still there?"

"I won't order you to do it."

"I'll go with you," Jacob said, speaking up before Cade could respond.

Cade smiled. "Damn, Jacob, how do you know I was going to say yes?"

"Weren't you?"

"Well, yeah, but it would have sounded braver for me to have volunteered rather than have you push me into it."

Jacob chuckled. "We could stand here and talk all day, or we could..."

"I thought you were going with me," Cade interrupted. "Why are you still here?"

Cade and Jacob climbed the wall, one advancing as the other covered for him until their leap-frogging brought them to the top. Here, they discovered several spent casings, so they knew they had reached the place where the Indians had been firing down on them.

They made it back to the bottom of the canyon much faster than it had taken them to climb up.

"Not an Indian in sight," Cade reported.

Mackenzie nodded, then called his officers together.

"Captain Beaumont, Lieutenant Boehm, take your companies to the bottom of the trail we used to come down and prevent any Indians from halting our egress. Captain Gunther, take H company to the top to prevent any Indians from coming down.

"Lieutenant Boyle, you take your company and do a reconnaissance of the village. I want everything you find destroyed," Mackenzie said.

As the men carried out their orders, they discovered that the Indians had been well prepared for winter. They found bows and arrows, newly-tanned buffalo robes, reservation-issued blankets, stone serving dishes, kettles, bolts of calico, and sacks of flour, cornmeal, and sugar, along with various other groceries.

"Look at this," Jacob said. "This may explain why they stopped shooting at us." He pointed to close to two dozen rifles and several cases of ammunition.

"I think the colonel will want to add these to our inventory," the lieutenant said.

For the next few hours, huge bonfires roared as the soldiers burned everything they found, including the tipis. When the destruction of the village was completed, Mackenzie turned his attention to the Indian horse herd the soldiers had captured.

"Do you have a count?" Mackenzie asked Lieutenant Jamison.

"Yes, sir. One thousand, two hundred and seventy-four horses, one hundred and fifty mules."

"Let the Seminole scouts pick out a hundred horses for their own use, and give Lawton his choice of what mules he might want to add to his teams."

"Yes, sir," Jamison said. "What about the rest of them?"

Mackenzie ran his hand through his hair, then made a decision he clearly didn't want to make.

"Shoot them."

"Sir?" Jamison was not sure he'd understood the command.

"Kill the rest of the horses, Lieutenant," Mackenzie said. "Kill every one of them."

Jamison shook his head. "The men aren't going to like this, Colonel."

"And I don't like giving the order, but it must be done."

"Yes, sir."

The gory job of killing the horses began. Firing squads executed the animals as fast as a troop of infantrymen could rope them and bring them into a killing pen. As the guns boomed and the herd grew smaller, the remaining horses became panicky and more difficult to handle.

Those men who weren't taking part in the killing of the horses stood guard against the possible return of any Indians. Many winced with almost every shot that was fired. These were men who not only lived on a day-to-day basis with horses, but they had grown up with them, and the death of every horse gnawed at their insides.

"Them horses knows what's happenin' to 'em 'n they don't like it," one of the troopers said.

"'Course they know it, cause horses is smart. Would you like it, if you was a horse?" another trooper asked.

"Hell, I don't like it, 'n I ain't a horse."

CADE COULD UNDERSTAND the reasoning behind the killing. To deny the Indians their mobility was to take away the opportunity for raiding, but still, he didn't like the wholesale destruction of the beautiful animals. He had seen hundreds of horses killed on the battlefields during the war, but those animals were victims of the war. Nobody had set out to deliberately kill them. These animals were being intentionally slaughtered.

Finally, by three o'clock in the afternoon, the grisly task was done, and Mackenzie led his men out of the canyon. Smoke from the burned village hung in the air, and already buzzards, wolves, and insects were being drawn to the unexpected feast lying in bloody piles behind them.

Mackenzie had lost only one man, Sergeant Major James Wilbur.

Nobody knew for sure how many Indians had been killed, although estimates ran as high as forty. But the victory, and victory it was, wasn't being measured by body count. Destroying the village the Indians had considered secure on the floor of Palo Duro Canyon had struck them a devastating blow.

Now, instead of being able to spend the winter in comfort and security, all the Indians—warriors, women, and children—would have to contend with blizzards and bitter cold without lodges, provisions, robes, or horses. Mackenzie knew this one battle would be the greatest motivator for the Indians to return to their reservations, and that was General Sheridan's intended result from this Red River Campaign.

21

"Mr. Harrison?" Sergeant Jackson said. Jackson was a member of D Troop, 10th Cavalry.

"Yes, Sergeant?"

"Some of the men and I was wonderin' if you'd say a few words over the Sergeant Major. I mean, seein' as how he seemed to set quite a store by you. Of course, you bein' a white man 'n all, you might not find it fittin'."

"I'd find it much more than fitting. I would find it an extreme honor to give a eulogy for the sergeant major."

Sergeant Jackson smiled and nodded his head. "I told the others I knowed you'd be more 'n proud to do it."

The grave was dug on the rim of the canyon, and although some suggested Sergeant Major Wilbur's body should be taken back to Fort Concho for burial, most believed this was a fitting place for him.

"We don't none of us know how long Fort Concho is goin' to be there," Sergeant Jackson said. "They's been other forts that just folded up 'n went away. But this here canyon is goin' to always be here, 'n by buryin' the sergeant major here, he'll always be able to look out over it."

Jacob, Cade, Colonel Mackenzie, Captain Beaumont, and nearly every other officer in Mackenzie's command attended the funeral of Sergeant Major James Wilbur. The men of D Troop stood at attention, unashamed of the tears that slid down their black cheeks.

Colonel Mackenzie was aware that Jacob had been asked to say a few words, and he had given his permission.

The Stars and Stripes were draped over a hastily-built coffin that had been made of ammunition crates, and it was at the head of this coffin that Jacob stood.

"I didn't know Sergeant Major Wilbur for very long, but ours was the kind of relationship that could and did put a lifetime of friendship into a few short months.

"Sergeant Major Wilbur died as he lived—a man of honor, duty, and courage. He died saving the life of an officer, a fellow soldier, a brother. He was proud of the Army he served, and as an outsider, I can easily see the Army was proud of him.

"When I first saw the crude coffin under this flag, my first thought was that this was wrong. Sergeant Major Wilbur should be buried in an oak casket trimmed with silver.

"Then I realized that this is the perfect casket for him. This coffin is made from ammunition crates. This coffin is, as Sergeant Major James Wilbur was, quintessentially Army."

Jacob put his hand on the coffin. "Rest in peace, my brave and noble friend. Your next reveille will be with the angels."

Jacob stepped back, and the bugler blew *Taps*. A salute was fired over the grave, and the coffin was lowered. Sergeant Jackson and another soldier folded the flag into a triangle so that only the blue field and white stars were showing, then each man from D Troop picked up a handful of dirt and threw it onto the casket.

"Your words were very moving," Cade said as he and Jacob walked away after the completion of the burial.

"They were heartfelt. Wilbur was a good man."

Cade nodded his head. "In a case like this, who'll get the flag?"

"Nobody," Jacob replied. "It'll stay with D Troop of the 10th."

"I thought the flag went to the family?"

"D Troop *was* Sergeant Major Wilbur's family."

After the funeral, Colonel Mackenzie moved his troops up Tule Creek to get away from the stench of the rotting carcasses. Bivouacking there, he sent out scouts every day, but only small bands of hostiles were found. After a few days of fruitless activity, it became evident that Mackenzie's Texas Campaign was about to come to an end.

Mackenzie sent for Cade and Jacob. When they stepped into the Sibley tent that was his headquarters, they saw two stools drawn up in front of his desk. There was a glass in front of each chair, and Mackenzie filled the glasses with brandy.

"Ranger Harrison, Mr. McCall, I called you in here to give you my personal thanks for the service both of you have provided. I couldn't have asked for more loyal or dedicated men, and I salute you." He held the glass out in front of him, then with a nod indicated that they too should drink.

Putting down his empty glass, he swept his hand in an invitation for the two men to be seated.

"This campaign will soon be coming to a close, and I've been informed that I'll be taking my command to Fort Sill. We'll stay out for a while longer, but only until the weather drives us into winter quarters. I'm assuming you, Mr. Harrison, will want to return to the Texas Rangers?"

"That's right. I'll be going back to Major Jones' company.

"And what about you, Mr. McCall?" Colonel Mackenzie asked. "You have a place in my command should you choose to stay with me."

"Colonel, it has been an honor serving with you, but if you are offering me the choice, I think I'd rather return to Colonel Miles and the friends I have there."

Mackenzie nodded. "I thought you might make that choice." He stood, and when he did, Cade and Jacob stood as well. "Gentlemen, again, I thank you for your service." He extended his hand across the desk to Cade and then Jacob. "If you leave today, you should be able to rejoin Miles sometime tomorrow. I believe the most recent courier message I received said he was camped on the Washita."

"So FORT SILL doesn't appeal to you," Jacob said after the two men had left Mackenzie's tent.

"Not particularly, especially if you're going back to the Rangers."

"Listen, Cade, when you get a chance, come see me. I'll be somewhere in Texas."

Cade laughed. "Thanks. That narrows it down quite a bit."

After saying goodbye to Captain Beaumont and the other friends he had made while serving with Mackenzie, Cade started back to rejoin General Miles. He couldn't help but compare the two officers as he rode. Mackenzie was a West Point graduate, and a brilliant officer who drove his men mercilessly. Despite that, he had their loyalty and respect because he drove himself just as hard.

Miles did not have the advantage of having attended the United States Military Academy, but had won his accolades on the field of battle. And like Mackenzie, Miles had the loyalty and respect of all who served under him, even those officers who were academy graduates and might have been resentful. The two senior officers didn't get along, perhaps because both were of such strong, independent natures.

"Hold up there, mister!" someone called, the shout pulling Cade from his reverie.

Looking toward the soldier who challenged him, Cade smiled. "Well, if it isn't Private Harrington."

"McCall? Is that you?"

"It is."

"Well, hell, we thought you'd deserted us. Gone over to scout for Mackenzie."

"I did, but now I'm back. Are you a picket, or part of a scouting party?"

"On a scout, sir. Lieutenant Baldwin is back a little ways. Billy Dixon is with us too."

Cade caught up with Billy, and the two rode together as the scouting patrol made its way back to General Miles' encampment.

"Is Mackenzie as big an ass as everybody think he is?" Billy asked.

"He's not at all. If I had to compare him to General Miles, I'd say they both have their strengths. But you'll never guess who was there with him."

Billy raised his eyebrows and shook his head.

"Jacob."

"What was he doing with Mackenzie?" Billy asked. "Everybody thought he was goin' off to Texas to join the Rangers."

"He did, and he's going back to the Rangers."

"I'll be damned," Billy said.

ONE OF THE first scouts Cade went out on after returning was with a young lieutenant who was leading a troop of twenty-five men. Lieutenant Farnsworth was in command of one of the many cavalry patrols that had been sent out by General Miles. After the rout at the Palo Duro, many of the Indians had been forced to return to the reservations, but others had defiantly chosen to band together and fight.

"I think we will find big band of dog soldiers," Brown Blackbird told Lieutenant Farnsworth. The Indian scout pointed to the head breaks of Sweetwater Creek. "Wait here, and I see."

"All right. Coyote Tail, you go with Brown Blackbird," Farnsworth said, addressing another scout.

Brown Blackbird shook his head. "No need. I go."

"Then we'll hold up here until you report back." He turned in his saddle to call out to his men.

"Dismount," he ordered. "While Brown Blackbird goes ahead, we can water our mounts."

The men dismounted and led their horses to the stream. Many of them filled their canteens as well.

ROBERT VAUGHAN

"Lieutenant!" one of the men shouted a moment later, and Farnsworth looked up to see a very large contingent of Indians bearing down on them.

"Get mounted!" Farnsworth shouted. "Densham, Hubbard, Ring, Jones, Taylor, Alcorn, with me. McCall, get the rest of the men under cover!"

Farnsworth and the six men with him provided covering fire as Cade led the rest of the soldiers across the creek, where they were able to take cover among the boulders that were scattered at the base of the hill. The noise of the gunfire was deafening, and a huge cloud of gun smoke drifted over the area. Densham and Hubbard went down and the other four were hit, but they were able to stem the advance of the Indians enough for the main body of soldiers to get into a more defensible position. The additional firepower turned the Indians away, and Farnsworth led the four men across the creek, joining the others.

After the Indians had withdrawn from the battlefield, Cade and Billy, with Private Smith and the buffalo wallow in their minds, crossed the creek and ran to the downed soldiers. Unfortunately, Densham and Hubbard were both dead.

"Where the hell was Brown Blackbird? Why didn't he warn us?" one of the soldiers said when several had joined Cade and Billy.

"He didn't warn us because he was one of 'em," Alcorn said. Alcorn was holding his hand over the bullet wound in his shoulder.

"How do you know he was one of them?" one of the other soldiers asked.

"Because he was part of the attack."

"I don't believe you," Lieutenant Farnsworth said. "Not Brown Blackbird."

"If you don't believe me, go right over there by that tree and you'll see him lying there."

"How do you know that's him?"

"Because I'm the one who killed the son of a bitch," Alcorn replied.

.   .   .

160

THE FARNSWORTH SCOUTING party pursued the fleeing hostiles for another couple of days, but when they had exhausted their rations, they returned to the main encampment.

Upon seeing Cade, Lieutenant Baldwin approached him. The expression on his face was grim.

"There's someone with the general we think you should meet," Baldwin said. The tone of Baldwin's voice both aroused Cade's curiosity and caused him concern.

"What is it, Frank?"

"I think it would be better if you see for yourself."

General Miles' Sibley tent was pitched on the bank of the Washita River. When Baldwin and Cade stepped into the headquarters, Cade saw someone with the general. He didn't recognize the man by name or face, but he did recognize the buckskin shirt and trousers and the Big 50 he carried, which told him this visitor was a buffalo hunter.

"Cade, this is W. F. Martin," General Miles said. Cade was surprised the general had called him by his first name, something he had never done before. That made him even more curious about this meeting.

"Mr. Martin is a buffalo hunter, and I'm going to let him tell you what he has told me," General Miles continued. "This is Cade McCall."

"It was awful, Mr. McCall," Martin began. "It was near 'bout the most awfulest thing I ever seen. Five of 'em it was, two men 'n three women, though one of the women warn't much more 'n a girl from all I could tell. They'd all been butchered up pretty much 'n the bodies had been some et, 'n they was all of 'em already gettin' most ripe. Besides which, one of the women was some burnt up."

Cade was curious about how this tragedy was connected to him.

"I don't know, but I'm afraid this massacre may have been committed against your friend, the man you knew at Douglass," General Miles said.

"Where did this happen?" Cade asked.

"They was up in Kansas on what they calls the old stage road. That's on the other side o' the Beaver River. A wagon it was, 'n it warn't only the people that was kilt. They kilt two cows, two calves, and the team of oxen. The oxen had been most et by the time I seen 'em, but they was both still in harness."

"What did you do with the bodies?" General Miles asked.

"I buried 'em. It's like I said, Gen'l, they had done got a might ripe. The only reason I've come to you with it is I figured there might be someone that should ought to know about it. I mean, what with the Injuns killin' a whole family like that."

"How many did you say there were?" Cade asked.

"They was five of 'em all told, two men 'n three women."

"Are you sure that was all? If I remember, the Germans had seven children. There should have been nine bodies."

"No, them five was all I found."

"Then what happened to the other four?" Lieutenant Baldwin asked.

"I think we all can guess," Cade said. "The bastards took four little girls."

His mind immediately flashed back to the capture of Isabella and Magnolia. The Indians had not kidnapped his wife and his friend, but when he heard that it was possible that these poor children were with the Indians, the pain was as great as it had been four years ago.

"This wagon was found in Kansas, which makes this atrocity within my area of responsibility. To that end, I'm going to send Lieutenant Henely and a detail to look into it."

"General, if possible, I'd like to be a part of that detail," Cade requested.

"You know this may not be the same wagon. It's possible these aren't your friends," General Miles said sympathetically.

"Yes, sir, I know. But I can't help but think it is."

"Then go with my blessing."

———

TWO DAYS LATER CADE, Lieutenant Henely, and six of Henely's

troopers had followed W.F. Martin to the site of the partially burned wagon.

The cattle and oxen were mostly bones by now, having been picked clean by wolves and buzzards.

"Even without the bodies, this is a gruesome sight," Henely said. "What do you think, Cade? Is this the same wagon that we came across before?

"I can't be certain, but I have a strong feeling it is."

"Let's sift through everything and see what we can find," Henely suggested.

As they began poking around in the scattered remains, Cade saw something he didn't want to see—a pile of ashes that would be unidentifiable, except for the six wire strings that had survived the fire. He remembered the pretty young girl who had entertained them with her beautiful voice and this very guitar.

"Cade, I just found something," Lieutenant Henely called.

"I did too. I'm pretty sure this is John's wagon," Cade replied, holding up the guitar strings. "Remember when one of the girls played the guitar for us? Of course, this could be a different guitar, but..."

"It's the same one," Henely said with grim certainty.

"How do you know?"

"Because I found their Bible," Henely said, holding up the book. "There's a name written in it."

"John German," Cade said. It wasn't a question, it was a statement.

"I'm sorry, Cade. It was your friend."

"Mr. Martin, are you absolutely certain there were only five bodies? Is it possible there may have been more, but they were scattered around by animals?"

"No, sir. I'm certain they was only five."

Cade took a deep breath.

"We'll never be able to know," Henely said. "It's been too long."

"Did you see any trail when you first discovered the wagon?" Cade asked.

"Yes, sir, they was some trail left when I first got here. It looked

163

like they went off that way," Martin replied, pointing to the southwest.

"Those poor little girls. How scared they must be," Henely said.

When Cade and Lieutenant Henely returned, they gave the grim report to General Miles that it was indeed the German wagon.

"Four of the girls are missing," Cade said. "And I have no doubt about what happened to them."

"I'll send a courier back to Camp Supply. From there, the information can be dispersed to every soldier still in the field," General Miles said. "I'll ask that the story be telegraphed to the Associated Press so that all the newspapers know the plight of those poor little girls. In the meantime, Lieutenant Henely, I'm charging you and Lieutenant Baldwin with the task of finding out what happened to the children." General Miles stopped talking for a moment, then continued, "And I mean whatever happened, be they dead or alive. Someone has to pay for this atrocity."

"Yes, sir. It is a mission that I shall gladly undertake. And Cade, you'll be the principal scout for this."

"Thank you," Cade replied.

ONE RESULT of everyone being informed about the German wagon incident was the interrogation of all the Indians who had surrendered to the reservations after the Palo Duro fight. A courier brought the news to General Miles that not one of them had any information about the missing children.

General Miles created a special task force whose primary purpose was to locate the German girls. He gave Lieutenant Baldwin overall command of the detachment, which included his scouts, Lieutenant Henely, and infantry, cavalry, a howitzer, and a supply train.

22

With Julia and Addie on the Plains

JULIA AND ADDIE HAD SURVIVED ON THEIR OWN FOR OVER SIX WEEKS, but as the autumn days got colder, they grew weaker with each passing hour.

One afternoon as they lay weak with exhaustion and hunger, three Indians happened across them. Dismounting, they came to examine the children.

"Bear Moccasin, look. It is not good that we have found white-eye children," one of the Indians said.

"We have found them, so it does not matter whether it is good or not."

"What will we do with them?" the third Indian asked.

"We should kill them," the other said.

"We will not kill them," Bear Moccasin said.

"Look at them. They will die whether we kill them or not."

"They will not die because we will take them with us."

"No."

"We will take them with us," Bear Moccasin insisted.

Because the three were holding their discussion in Cheyenne, neither Julia nor Addie had any idea what they were saying. But even if they could have understood that their fate was being decided, it would have had little impact on them. By now, the two sisters were in such dire straits that the unexpected appearance of the Indians neither frightened them nor gave them hope for survival. Julia stared at the three with almost complete indifference.

One of the Indians spoke to the girls, but they couldn't understand him. Then another spoke to them in English.

"Who are you?"

"I am Julia, and this is my sister Addie. Who are you?"

"I am Bear Moccasin. Why are you here?"

"Where is Catherine? Where is Sophia?"

"Why are you here?" Bear Moccasin repeated.

"Indians killed Mama and Papa. And then they killed Stephen and Rebecca and Joanna," Julia told him.

"Then they took me and Julia," Addie said. "And Catherine and Sophia."

"But they rode away on their ponies and left us here," Julia added.

The Indians began having an animated discussion, speaking in their own language. The one who had identified himself as Bear Moccasin would frequently point to Julia and her sister, so she knew they were talking about them.

"You come," Bear Moccasin said.

Julia and Addie both tried to stand, but they could not.

"You come!" Bear Moccasin said more insistently. Then he and one of the other Indians lifted the girls onto their ponies, and once that was done, they rode away. They had barely started when Julia fell from the pony. She was picked up and put on the pony again, this time riding in front.

The three Indians rode until after dark, when they reached a village. There was much wailing going on because they were mourning the deaths of six warriors who had been killed that day in a battle with soldiers.

"Why have you brought these to us?" Whirlwind asked.

"Because we found them," Bear Moccasin replied.

"You should have left them. They will be trouble for us," Whirlwind said.

"Whirlwind does not think before he speaks," Grey Beard said. "If the soldiers see us with the white-eye children, they will shoot at us. If the soldiers see us without the white-eye children, they will shoot at us. It will not matter whether we have the children or not."

"They are very weak," Bear Moccasin said. "I think that they will die without food."

"Feed them," Grey Beard ordered.

Again, although Julia realized they must be talking about her and her sister, she couldn't understand them.

"We will give you food," Bear Moccasin said.

"Thank you." Julia attempted a smile, but her face was so emaciated, she could not force her muscles to work.

Bear Moccasin cut some very thin strips of raw buffalo meat and offered it to them, but although they both tried, they were unable to swallow it. Then Bear Moccasin smiled. Picking up a stick, he dipped it a into a leather pouch. When he withdrew the stick, honey was dripping from the end of it. He gave it first to the smaller of the two girls, then to the larger one.

"Oh, yes, thank you. It is very good!" Julia said.

Addie was too weak to comment.

After both girls had sucked on the stick with the honey, Bear Moccasin took them into a tipi where a woman was tending a fire. They laid down on a buffalo hide, and soon fell into an exhausted sleep.

VERY EARLY THE NEXT MORNING, Julia and Addie were awakened by the smell of cooking food. The woman handed each of them a thin strip of meat, and this time, the girls were able to eat it.

After they had eaten, Bear Moccasin and his woman wrapped them in blankets and took them to Grey Beard's encampment on

North McClellan Creek. They were surprised to see falling snowflakes. Julia drew the blanket tighter. No matter what was going to happen to them, she was glad Bear Moccasin had found them before it snowed.

When they got to the encampment, Julia was taken into one tipi, but Addie was not. She did not have the energy to protest, and soon she was lying before a fire, her eyelids too heavy to stay open.

With Sophia

SOPHIA HAD NOT SEEN Catherine since she was taken from Medicine Water's village, and although she realized there was a possibility she would never see her again, she couldn't let herself think that. Catherine now occupied the same place in her thoughts, prayers, and heart as did Julia and Addie. Until she knew for sure what had happened to them, Sophia would hold onto the hope and the belief that all three of her surviving sisters were still alive.

A warrior came into her tipi, and she braced herself. She had already been subjected to the same indignities as had been visited upon Catherine, and before Catherine, Rebecca. She closed her eyes, clenched her fists, and waited.

"Come," the warrior said.

Sophia opened her eyes with the thought that maybe he was not going to do anything to her. At least, none of the previous incidents had started this way.

"Come," the warrior said again.

Sophia got up from her pallet and followed the warrior, whose name she didn't know, to another tipi. Here, Buffalo Robe was waiting for her. Although Buffalo Robe had shared her with a couple of the others, he had not touched her. In fact, his treatment of her had been much better than she had expected.

"Come and see," Buffalo Robe said, opening the gap in the tent so she could step inside. Although some light came down through the opening at the top of the tipi, it was still dim inside, so at first, she wasn't certain what she was seeing.

"Belong to you," Buffalo Robe said, pointing to a figure lying on a buffalo robe.

Sophia shook her head. "Belongs to me? What do you mean, belongs to me?"

"Sophia?" said a very weak voice.

"Oh, my goodness!" Sophia hurried to kneel beside the emaciated figure. "Julia, is that you?" Tears began streaming down her face. "I can't believe I'm seeing my little sister. How did you get here?"

"Some Indians found us," Julia answered, her voice barely a whisper.

"Us? Addie is here, too?"

"Yes, but I don't know where she is now."

"Where have you been all this time?"

"Out there," Julia replied, pointing.

"With the Indians?"

"No, just with Addie."

"You two were all alone? Weren't you afraid?"

"Not in the daytime," Julia said, "but at night the wolves came. Addie wanted to cry, but I told her if she did, the wolves might eat us."

"Oh, Julia, you are the bravest person I know."

Sophia pulled her sister to her into a loving embrace. When she did so, she could feel how terribly frail she was.

With Cade

IT WAS A COLD NOVEMBER MORNING, and Lieutenant Baldwin and his task force had been in the field for almost two weeks. Baldwin got his men underway just before six o'clock and Cade, who had gone out half an hour earlier, was about two miles north of the others. He had just come up on a ridge when he saw something ahead.

Reaching into his saddlebag, Cade pulled out his telescope, slid it open, and held it to his eye. After he adjusted the focus, he saw from one to two hundred lodges and as many as five or six hundred ponies. Closing his telescope, he jerked his horse around and galloped back toward Baldwin and the main group.

"Damn, Cade, what's got you in such a hurry this morning?"

"There's a big village ahead," Cade said.

"How big?"

"I'd say well over a hundred lodges, maybe as many as two hundred. They're on the north side of McClellan Creek."

"Lead the way," Baldwin said. "Bugler, sound assembly."

Keeping Cade with him, he directed the rest of his scouts to move well out on each flank. Lieutenant Henely sent ten of his men forward as skirmishers, while six men were assigned as rear guard. As soon as this was done, the detachment of about a hundred men got underway, moving as rapidly as possible over the broken terrain rising before them. When they came within five hundred yards of the Indian encampment, the infantry formed a line to the right and the cavalry formed a line to the left. The single howitzer was brought up to the middle.

GREY BEARD WAS LYING on a flat rock high atop a precipice that guarded the entrance into the breaks. Like Cade, Grey Beard had a telescope, and with the advantage of elevation, he was able to see the troops advancing on his village.

Grey Beard had prepared for this contingency, and his escape route was well planned. He would take his people across the barren plains, where his band could capture more horses. There they would settle into a canyon, where they could spend the winter while waiting for spring, when the grass would grow and forage would be plentiful.

He hurried back to the village to order a retreat.

. . .

"LITTLE SQUAW, WHAT IS HAPPENING?" Catherine asked anxiously when Little Squaw came into the lodge.

"Soldiers come," Little Squaw said.

"I'll be freed," Catherine replied, excited by the prospect.

Little Squaw had a sad expression on her face.

"Grey Beard says you must come with us."

A warrior by the name of Standing Bear came into the lodge again and, seeing Little Squaw, shouted angrily at her.

"Why are you here? I will be in charge of this white-eye. We go now."

"Where are we going?" Catherine asked.

"Where I go, you will go," Standing Bear said.

Standing Bear grabbed Catherine and pushed her outside. There she saw that Sophia was already mounted. This was the first time she had seen Sophia since they had been separated.

"Sophia," Catherine called, her happiness at the reunion temporarily overriding her worry about what was happening to them now.

"Catherine, I saw Julia."

"Julia is alive?"

"Yes, and Addie, too," Sophia said.

"Get on horse," Standing Bear ordered.

"Where are they?" Catherine asked as she mounted.

"I don't know now, but they're here somewhere, I think."

"Stone Eagle, find the little ones and shoot them," Standing Bear ordered.

"I will do so," Stone Eagle replied.

"No, don't, please don't hurt them!" Catherine begged. Although the order and response had been given in Cheyenne, by now Catherine could speak enough of the language that she had understood what was being said.

"Catherine, what is it?" Sophia asked, frightened by Catherine's words.

"They're going to kill Julia and Addie!"

Before Sophia could reply, there was a huge bang as a howitzer shell exploded in the village.

"Soldiers are using guns that shoot twice!" one of the warriors said, using their term for artillery. "We must run!"

Almost immediately after the exploding howitzer round, Catherine heard *Charge* being played on a bugle. She had no way of recognizing the bugle call, but she did understand its significance. It meant the Army had arrived.

Even as she thought that, total pandemonium erupted. The village echoed with the sound of gunfire from rifles and howitzers, the bugle calls, the thunder of hoofbeats, the shouting and yelling of both Indians and soldiers, and the screams and cries of the women and children.

"Go, you go!" Standing Bear shouted, striking her pony with a three-foot-long piece of rope. She and Sophia were rushed away, and as they left, Catherine looked behind her. That was when she saw Stone Eagle lying dead. She breathed a prayer of thankfulness that he had been killed before he could shoot Julia and Addie, then added a quick prayer for forgiveness, for feeling pleasure over someone's death.

The Indians who were riding with the two girls urged their horses into a gallop, and the sounds of the battle receded behind them.

23

CADE WAS WITH THE VANGUARD OF THE ADVANCING TROOPS. NOT ALL of the Indians had fled. Several had remained behind to protect the withdrawal of the others. They put up a spirited fight for a brief period of time, then those who hadn't been killed threw down their weapons and held up their hands.

"Gather up the equipage and burn the lodges!" Baldwin ordered.

"Frank, no!" Cade shouted, using Baldwin's first name in his excitement.

"What? Why not?"

"We need to search for the girls."

"Yes, yes, of course. I wasn't thinking," Baldwin replied. "All right, men, search all the lodges, but be careful there isn't some warrior hiding in one of them."

There were almost two hundred tipis to examine, and it was ten minutes into the search before one of the soldiers called out, "Lieutenant, there's somethin' in this here 'n."

"Wait," Baldwin replied, and he, Cade, and Billy Dixon hurried over to it.

"What did you find?" Cade asked.

"Looked to me like they was somethin' a' movin' under them buffalo robes there." The soldier pointed.

"It's got to be a Injun, else why is he hidin'?" one of the others said.

"Let me pull the robe aside, but be ready," Cade said.

Cade jerked the robe aside. There he saw a child, so emaciated and dressed in such rags that he wasn't immediately aware that she was even a white girl, let alone one the German girls.

"Do you speak English, honey?" Cade asked. "What's your name?"

"Mr. McCall, you know who I am. My name's Julia German," she replied as she tried to smile.

"Of course I know you, darlin'," Cade said, wrapping his arms around her and pulling her to him. He could feel his eyes welling over with tears, but he felt no embarrassment, because when he looked up, both Billy Dixon and Lieutenant Baldwin were showing the same emotion.

"Have you got anything to eat?" Julia asked.

"Here's another one!" a soldier shouted, and when Cade carried Julia outside, he saw one of the other soldiers holding a child who was even younger than Julia.

A few minutes later, both Julia and Addie were wrapped in blankets and sitting on a buffalo robe. There were a dozen biscuits left over from breakfast, and the cook had spread them with apple butter and given them to the girls. Julia and Addie ate their fill.

"Do you know where your sisters are?" Cade asked. He had hesitated to question them until he felt they understood that they were now safe.

"I seen Sophia," Julia said, "and she said Catherine was here too. When the shootin' started, an Indian came and took Sophia away."

"Then thank God, we know they're still alive," Baldwin said.

"At least for now," one of the other soldiers said, and his comment was met with a disapproving glare from Cade.

"I tell you what," one of the troopers said. "I've been running around out here for three months, but I'll stay out until doomsday if it takes that long to get them other two girls back."

"Get Dr. Powell up here," Baldwin ordered.

A few minutes later, the regimental surgeon arrived and got his first look at Julia and Addie.

"Oh, God in heaven," he said.

"What can you do for them, Doc?" Cade asked.

Watching the two little girls devouring the biscuits, Dr. Powell shook his head. "It looks to me like the most crucial thing is being taken care of right now. They're terribly undernourished. It'll also help to get them cleaned up and in some clean clothes."

Julia and Addie were still wearing the same dresses they had been wearing when captured. Besides being filthy from over two months of exposure, the dresses were badly torn, exposing bare skin in many places.

"Where are we going to get clothes for a couple of little girls?" one of the troopers asked.

"Murchison," another responded.

"What?"

"Murchison used to be a tailor. We could gather up a couple of clean flour sacks, 'n Murchison could make dresses for 'em. And we'll see if we can find somethin' around here he could use to sew up coats."

"Good idea," Dr. Powell said. "And Frank, have the cook heat up some water for me." Dr. Powell pointed to the tipi that had been identified as the one belonging to Gray Wolf. "I'll get a fire going, and we'll get them cleaned up."

"And can you trim their fingernails?" Billy Dixon asked. "Bless their little hearts, their hands look like bird claws."

By now the supply wagons had been brought up, and Cade began looking them over.

"What ya looking for, Mr. McCall?" Sergeant Scott asked. Scott was the cook.

"The little girls are too frail to ride a horse. I want to put them in a wagon if I can find one with enough room."

"Put them in the kitchen wagon," Sergeant Scott said. "I'll make enough room for 'em."

"Cade, you'd better get out here!" Dixon called. "Looks like the Indians want another go at us."

There were about forty mounted Indians coming toward the village from which they had so recently retreated. With shouts and gunfire, they made what was little more than a feint, then withdrew. Five minutes later, they charged again, coming much closer than they had before. This time, however, when they withdrew, they left three of their number dead on the field.

With Catherine

THE URGENCY of the Indian retreat meant Standing Bear, who was riding alongside Catherine, had to use his rope's end to force her pony into a gallop. Because of that, she was riding faster than she had ever ridden before, and she struggled to hang on to the galloping horse.

Catherine was fighting conflicting emotions. She was happy the soldiers had come, but she was disappointed that she and Sophia had been forced to leave with the Indians. Had they been allowed to stay in the camp, they would have been rescued by now.

As they were leaving, Sophia had said she had seen Julia, and Julia had said that Addie was there, too. Catherine was sure she had understood when Standing Bear ordered Stone Eagle to kill Julia and Addie, but when she looked back, she thought it was Stone Eagle who was lying on the ground.

Had Stone Eagle been able to pass Standing Bear's order on to someone else? She prayed fervently that Julia and Addie were still alive, but she feared they were not. If the Indians hadn't killed them, what was to keep the soldiers from doing so? Who knew anything about the plight of four children whose parents and siblings had been killed so many weeks ago?

During the escape, they crossed and re-crossed the Red River several times. Catherine found herself wondering about Sophia. She had seen her as they were fleeing the village, but she hadn't seen her since. Had the fleeing Indians split into several parties? And if so, was she with one of the other parties?

The Indians made camp in one of the ravines that led off from the Red River. It was big enough to accommodate all the horses, and unless someone actually came into it, they wouldn't see them. Because there had been such pandemonium when they fled the site on McClellan Creek, all the lodge poles and skins had been left behind.

That night a terrible storm came. Lightning flashes filled the sky, the thunder roared as loudly as the howitzer had been, the wind howled, and the rain came down in torrents. It rained so hard that the bottom of the ravine began filling with water.

The rain was very cold, so cold that Catherine feared it would soon turn into freezing rain or even sleet. To make it worse, with the water now several inches deep, it was impossible to lie down or even to sit.

Little Squaw came to her, bringing dry moccasins and a buffalo robe.

"Thank you. My feet are freezing," Catherine said as she moved onto a boulder to put on the moccasins. Little Squaw then gave her a poncho made out of gutta-percha cloth. It was clearly marked as belonging to the U.S. Army.

"Is Sophia with us?"

Little Squaw shook her head.

"What about my little sisters? Are they here?" Catherine asked.

"They did not come."

"Are they dead?"

"I do not know. Come," Little Squaw said, taking Catherine's hand and leading her from one boulder to another.

Catherine had no idea where Little Squaw was taking her, but of all the Indians she had encountered, Little Squaw had been the nicest to her. As she thought about it, Little Squaw had been more than just nice; she had more than likely saved Catherine's sanity, if not her life.

177

Catherine followed her until they reach a depression in the bank. For a moment she didn't quite understand what Little Squaw, who was smiling so proudly, was pointing out to her, Then, with a happy little gasp, she knew what it was. She could put her buffalo robe into the depression, and it would make a bed out of the water.

"Oh, Little Squaw, thank you so much!" Catherine was grateful to Little Squaw, not only for finding a place for her to rest, but also for being a friend when she so desperately needed one.

In a totally unplanned and spontaneous moment, Catherine gave Little Squaw a hug and a kiss on the cheek. Little Squaw returned the hug, then she found a nearby depression where she too burrowed into the wall of the ravine.

As Catherine pulled her buffalo around her, she prayed a prayer of thanksgiving for Little Squaw. She also prayed that Sophia was somewhere safe and dry. As for her little sisters, she uttered the same prayer she had said every night since September 11th: let them be safe.

The rain had now turned to sleet and continued to fall, but an exhausted Catherine slept.

The Baldwin Bivouac

BECAUSE THE WAGONS had been brought up, almost every soldier in Baldwin's task force had been able to climb under the tarpaulins and get out of the rain. The men who were on guard duty had to endure the storm, but that was only for two hours until they were replaced by the next relief.

Baldwin was certain the Indians would not try another attack. For one thing, in their hasty retreat, the Indians had left many of their weapons behind them, and they would know they were outgunned. The other reason was the severe ice storm that was now pelting the animals. He didn't expect that many Indians would venture out.

. . .

CADE STUCK his head into the kitchen wagon. A kerosene lantern was burning very low, but in its dim glow, he was able to see both little girls sleeping. He climbed up into the wagon with them and tied the canvas down behind him to keep the sleet from coming in. With everything made secure, he laid down near the tailgate, extinguished the lantern, and with a prayer for the safety and eventual recovery of Catherine and Sophia, let the pitter-patter of the sleet put him to sleep.

With Catherine

WHEN THE INDIANS left their encampment the next morning, Standing Bear was yelling at Catherine with such anger and ferocity that she failed to tighten the cinch to her saddle. As a result, when she tried to mount, the saddle slid to the side, and she fell.

Instead of helping her to her feet, Standing Bear began beating her with the same rope's end he had been using on the horses. Catherine wrapped her arms around her legs and coiled up to protect herself from the painful lashes.

"Do not make me slow. If you do, I will kill you as I killed your little sisters."

"Oh!" she cried, not so much from pain as hearing that Julia and Addie had been killed. Standing Bear had said that he had killed them, but Catherine didn't believe he had done the deed himself since he had been riding beside her for most of the escape. But he *had* ordered Stone Eagle to kill them. Maybe he did not know that Stone Eagle had been hit when the soldiers had fired on the camp.

Then Catherine heard Little Squaw's voice. She knew it was Little Squaw, but she had never heard such anger in her voice before.

"Standing Bear, you are a snake. A man of evil, and you shame me for ever having given birth to you. Stop this now. Do not hit this woman one more time!"

Mercifully, the beating stopped, and Catherine opened her eyes to see Standing Bear walking away, holding the piece of rope in his hand. Little Squaw was standing there with her hands on her hips, glaring at him. Then, turning to look down at Catherine, the expression on her face softened.

"Little Squaw?" Catherine said, more stunned by what she had just seen than hurt by the whipping.

Little Squaw reached down, helped Catherine to her feet, wiped away the tears, then kissed her.

"Standing Bear said he killed Julia and Addie," Catherine said. "Is that true?"

"I do not know if it true. It may be he said such a thing to make you feel bad. I am sorry my son beat you," Little Squaw said. "He will not do it again."

"Standing Bear is your son?"

"Yes."

Because of the one-word response, Catherine realized Little Squaw did not want to talk about it, so she asked no more questions.

Little Squaw helped Catherine put the saddle back on her horse and draw the cinch tight. Just before Catherine was about to mount, Little Squaw put her hand on Catherine's shoulder.

"I think you will see Sophia soon."

"You have seen her?" Catherine asked excitedly.

"I have not, but I know she is safe."

"Thank you, Little Squaw. I will never forget you."

24

After leaving Grey Beard's village, Baldwin and his men returned to General Miles' bivouac on the Washita. The general was apprised of the recovery of the two children. It was when General Miles went to the field infirmary that anyone thought to ask the girls where they had been for two months. It had been surmised that their condition was a result of miscreant behavior imposed upon them by their Indian captors.

When everyone learned that a seven-year-old and a five-year-old had survived on their own, living off roots, berries, and leftovers from abandoned Army encampments, there was a renewed energy to go after the remaining hostiles.

"As long as there's a single Indian in the Red River Valley, I vow to chase them until every one of them is forced to live the way these two little girls have been living," General Miles said. "They expect us to go in for the winter? Well, I'll stay in the field, no matter how cold or how far we have to travel until the last Indian is either dead or on a reservation."

"We'll be right there beside you," Lieutenant Baldwin said.

"Remember, we think there are still two girls out there," Lieutenant Henely said.

"We won't forget them," General Miles said. "Right now, I think these two little ones should go to Fort Leavenworth. My wife is there, and I will ask her to oversee their care and recovery as much as possible."

"Do you think they are up to the rigors of traveling that far?" Cade asked.

"We'll do it in stages. I think they should stay here for a few days, then they can be moved to Camp Supply," Dr. Powell said. "But I think after a few days of rest and good food, they might be ready."

"All right, you're the doctor," Miles said. "We can keep them here until you say they're ready to go."

During the time the little girls were with Doctor Powell, Baldwin and his scouts, including Cade and Billy, were making daily patrols to ensure no Indians were in a position to launch a surprise attack on them. They were also trying to locate Grey Beard and his band, where they believed they would find the two older sisters.

The scouts who were sent out believed they could cover more ground if they separated. As a result, although they left camp together and arranged for a rendezvous point before returning to camp, each was essentially alone during each scout.

It was on the third day of solo patrolling that Cade saw three Indians. In truth, the three Indians saw him, because his first awareness of their presence was when he heard the whizz of an arrow that flashed by just a few inches from his face.

Looking in the direction from which the arrow had come, Cade saw the warriors, none of whom were mounted. One Indian was reaching for another arrow, and the other two were armed with lances. Cade didn't find that particularly unusual, knowing that many of their weapons had been abandoned when they fled the village.

The Indian armed with the bow managed to get a second arrow nocked and drew back the string. Cade didn't want to kill these men, because he wanted to see if they could give him any information that would lead to Grey Beard and the two girls.

Cade's hesitation almost cost him his life when the warrior loosed the bowstring and the arrow plunged into Cade's leg just above his knee.

Thinking they now had the advantage, the two Indians who were armed with lances charged toward him. He wasn't their prime target because he was still mounted, but if they killed his horse, he would be very vulnerable.

Cade had no choice but to pull his pistol and fire. His first two shots brought down the charging warriors, and his third shot killed the bowman as he was nocking yet a third arrow.

Cade put his pistol back in the holster, then, with a quiet grunt of pain, he broke off the arrow shaft so the wound wouldn't worsen on the ride back. When he looked at the wound, there didn't appear to be that much blood, but he felt that if he pulled the arrow out, it might exacerbate the wound. He also might separate the shaft from the arrowhead, leaving it embedded in his leg, which would make it even worse. He decided to leave it there until he got back to the encampment, but before he left, he found one of the other scouts and told him he was heading back so they didn't waste precious time looking for him when he missed the rendezvous.

THAT EVENING CADE was sitting on the ground, leaning against a wagon wheel with his bandaged leg stretched out in front of him. Dr. Powell had told him he had made the correct decision by leaving the arrowhead in until he got back. Removing the arrowhead had reopened the wound, and it was more painful coming out than it had been going in. The doctor had given him some laudanum and that had helped, but now he was treating his pain with coffee sweetened with more than a little whiskey.

"How's the leg feeling?" Lieutenant Baldwin asked as he came toward him. Taking a seat on the ground, Baldwin handed Cade a biscuit filled with bacon. "I figured you might not feel like walking over to get your supper, so I brought it to you."

"Thanks."

"Since these two little girls seem to trust you more than anybody else, General Miles would like for you to go with them to Camp Supply," Baldwin told Cade. "And anyway, Doctor Powell thinks you ought to see the post surgeon there. He's worried your leg might start to fester."

"My leg's fine," Cade said, taking another drink from his cup.

"You do remember what happened to Amos Chapman, don't you?" Baldwin asked, reminding Cade of their mutual friend who had lost his leg at the Buffalo Wallow fight.

"I remember."

"Well, good, that's settled. Tomorrow, we'll send you in the ambulance with Julia and Addie."

DR. POWELL, Cade, the two little girls, and the four soldiers who were sent along to provide protection left the bivouac early the next morning. The trip to Camp Supply would take three days, and while they camped the first night out on the trail, the second night they were able to stay at the Polly Hotel, which was a stage waystation.

Mrs. Polly tried to engage the girls in conversation, but they cowered in the corner. When she tried to coax them to the table, they wouldn't come, so Cade took their beans and cornbread and sat down on the floor beside them. Instead of using a utensil, the girls picked up each bean with her fingers. It was then that Cade noticed something black under Julia's fingernail. Taking her hand in his, he looked more closely.

"What happened?" he asked.

"They put sticks," Julia said. "And here and here." She pointed to scars between her fingers and around her eyes.

"Why did they do that?" Cade asked.

Julia raised her eyebrows but didn't answer.

"Then they burned 'em," Addie said, showing Cade her scars as well.

"The bastards," Cade said, immediately sorry he had cursed in front of the girls. What all had these little girls survived? Someday he would like to hear their story, but not now. He understood how fragile they were, and how long it would take for them to recover their physical health, and more importantly, their mental health.

BECAUSE THEY WERE NO LONGER in danger of an Indian attack, two of the soldiers from the escort detail rode ahead to Camp Supply to take the news of the rescue of the two little girls.

Camp Supply was a secure base, surrounded by stockade walls with bastions at the corners. The gates were open wide to allow the ambulance to enter, and it was met by Colonel Alfred Sully, the post commandant.

Colonel Sully wasn't the only one there to meet them. They were given a warm welcome by the women of the post, but in deference to the girls' fragility, they were allowed to stay with Dr. Powers and Cade in the post hospital.

"WERE you able to remove the arrowhead?" Dr. Waters asked Dr. Powell as he went to take a look at the wound in Cade's leg.

"Yes, I was."

"Good, good," Dr. Waters said as he removed the bandage. He examined the wound carefully. "I think we'll be able to save the leg if he doesn't get sepsis."

Then the doctor addressed Cade specifically. "That's a real possibility, you know."

Cade was startled by Dr. Waters' comment, even though Lieutenant Baldwin had reminded him that Amos Chapman had lost his leg due to a similar wound. Of course, in Chapman's case, his wound had been exposed to muddy water and the elements for several days with the bullet still in his leg. The arrowhead had been taken from Cade's leg the same day.

"Well, let's just do what we can so I don't get this sepsis," Cade said. "I'm not letting you take off my leg."

Dr. Waters laughed. "That's what they all say, but in the end, everybody does what they have to do to stay alive." He reached for a bottle of carbolic acid. "This may sting a bit."

WITH CADE'S wound attended to, he went to the room where the girls were staying. Dr. Waters' wife was sitting with them. She had brought new dresses that the officers' wives club had sewn for them, but so far, Julie and Addie wouldn't accept them.

"Mr. McCall, I'm so glad you're here," Mrs. Waters said. "These poor little souls. Maybe they would have been better served to have been left behind. Will they ever get over the atrocities that have been visited upon them?"

"I can't believe you said that," Cade said as he moved toward the girls. "I'm going to have to ask you to leave." Cade put his arms around the girls and pulled them close to him.

Mrs. Waters took out a handkerchief and began wiping her eyes. "What I said is true. How will they ever forget what those savages did to them?"

"They never will, but if they find people who will treat them with compassion instead of contempt, they'll have a chance. And now, good day, Mrs. Waters."

When she was gone, Cade turned his attention to the girls.

"Look at these pretty dresses. Which one do you want to put on first?"

Neither girl said anything.

"All right. I like the red-checked ones, so let's put those on first."

"I like blue," Julia said.

Cade smiled. "Then blue it is."

CADE STAYED at Camp Supply for a few days, ostensibly to make certain infection didn't set in, but in reality, he stayed to make certain there wasn't a repeat of the scene with Mrs. Waters.

He thought about John German, a man whom he had met at a time in his life when he might have been at his lowest. Until he had run across the wagon moving through Kansas, Cade had known absolutely nothing about the man, and now he felt a kinship with these two little girls that would probably exist for the rest of his life.

"I feel like the girls are stable enough to go on to Fort Leavenworth," Dr. Powers said. "I don't suppose you'd go with me all the way?"

Cade took a deep breath. "I am not the person to take guardianship of these children if that's what you're suggesting. I have a soon-to-be-four-year-old step-daughter in Dodge City, and a five-year-old..." Cade hesitated before he referenced Stone Forehead, "nephew in Tennessee. If I was going to become a parent, I'd adopt the two kids I already have."

"But these children! They have become dependent upon you, Cade."

"All right. I'll go with you as far as Dodge City, but then I have to get back to General Miles. The greatest gift I can give Julia and Addie is to help find their big sisters."

"I can accept that," Dr. Powers said. "We plan to leave the day after tomorrow."

TWO DAYS LATER, an Army ambulance was assigned to take the girls to Dodge. The ambulance was different from the other Army wagons in that it had a completely enclosed body, and with the weather quite cold now, it would make for a more comfortable ride. With an escort of four soldiers plus Cade, the ambulance detail started north.

It was about a hundred-mile trip, and they planned to make Dodge City in four days. However, the second day out they were caught in a blizzard, the heavy snowflakes coming down so thick and so fast they could only see a few feet in front of them. Finally, they were forced to come to a stop and wait the storm out.

With the driver, Dr. Powell, Cade, and the four escort troopers, plus Julia and Addie, it was very crowded inside the ambulance, but the combined body heat of all nine of them helped keep them warm during the storm.

"Dr. Powell says we're going to ride on a train," Julia told Cade as she and Addie sat next to him.

"That's right."

"I've never been on a train before. Have you?"

"Yes, lots of times."

"Is it scary?"

Cade smiled and put his hand gently on Julia's cheek. "Sweetheart, after all you've been through, I don't think anything will ever scare you again. But you'll like riding on the train. It's fun."

"Will you go with us?" she asked.

"Not this time, little one, but I'll come and see you." He started to add that he would bring Catherine and Sophia back to them, but he thought better of that. It would not be good to give them false hope.

"Do you promise?" Addie's eyes were clouded with tears.

"I promise," Cade said as he kissed the child on the forehead. He hoped he could keep that promise as he shifted his leg, reminding himself of how easily things could change.

THE NEXT MORNING, they were greeted by a blue sky and a world of white. The snow was so deep that the road they had been following was no longer visible, so the escort troopers rode in front to break the snow and find the road. As they got closer to Dodge City, other traffic had been using the road, so it was easy to find their way.

When they reached Dodge City, the troopers and the ambulance and driver went straight to Fort Dodge. Cade remained at the depot with Dr. Powell and the two girls as they waited for the train that would take them to Fort Leavenworth. The two wood-burning stoves in the depot put out a blanket of warmth that was greatly appreciated by Cade, and especially by Julia and Addie.

Cade waited with them until the train arrived, then he walked to the train with them to tell them goodbye. Just before they got onto the train, first Julia and then Addie hugged Cade.

"Thank you for saving us from the Indians," Julia said.

Cade couldn't answer, so he knelt beside them and hugged them once more. Finally, kissing each child, he let them go.

He waved as he stood on the platform, watching the train as it departed. He stayed there, staring at the empty track until the train was out of sight because he didn't want anyone to see the tears that had welled up in his eyes.

Turning away from the track, Cade looked out over the town that had been so much a part of his recent life.

Front Street and First Avenue were busy with traffic, wagons, buckboards, and surreys moving people and freight back and forth. Pedestrians were going in and out of the businesses along Front Street: Isaac Young's harness shop, Herman Fringer's apothecary, the Post Office, Rath and Company, O.K. Clothing Store, Daniel Wolf's General Store, and yes, the sign for Harrison and McCall Freighting Company.

He saw two little girls about the ages of Julia and Addie. They were walking on each side of their mother, holding onto her hands. The striking difference between this peaceful scene and what he now knew it had been like for Julia and Addie made him take a deep breath.

Cade closed his eyes and stood there for a moment, then he shook his head.

No, I can't dwell on this. If I can't put this behind me, how will Julia and Addie ever be able to do it?

Clearing his mind, he started toward the Red House, and just seeing it, even before he went inside, had some therapeutic effect. With a genuine smile on his face, he pushed through the batwing doors.

. . .

"CADE MCCALL!" Jeter called happily when he saw Cade. "We thought you were running around somewhere down in Texas! What brings you home?"

"I thought I might come here and visit a while, but if you'd rather me be running around down in Texas, I suppose I could go back," Cade teased.

"What? No, don't be silly. Come over here and have a drink. What'll you have? Whiskey?"

"Yes, whiskey, if you would pour it in a cup of hot coffee."

Jeter chuckled. "Cold, are you?"

"Yeah. There was a time last summer when I thought I'd never be cold again. Boy, was I wrong."

"Just a minute. Wait until I get Magnolia out here. She'll be mighty glad to see you."

"Oh, Cade!" Magnolia called a moment later, rushing to him with her arms spread wide. "You're back!"

"How's the prettiest woman in Dodge City?" Cade asked, grinning broadly as they embraced.

"You're going to stay with us awhile, aren't you?" Magnolia asked.

"Not too long," Cade told her.

"Well, I hope you're here long enough to come by the house and see us and have a good meal or two."

"I'll be there. I can't wait to see all my girls."

With General Miles

"It's good to see ya back and still with two legs," Billy said when Cade returned.

"It'll take more than a Comanche arrowhead to put me down," Cade replied as he shook hands with his friend. "Any news from Grey Beard since I've been gone?"

"So far, nothin' good, but maybe there's somethin' goin' on now. General Miles called a big meetin' with all his officers and scouts for one o'clock. You got back just in time."

"Negotiations are not going well," General Miles said at the meeting. "The agencies have sent out couriers to all the renegades, begging them to come into the reservations, but so far, very few have accepted the invitation. As I have said many times before, I intend to stay in the field until there is a resolution to the status of the other two German girls. I intend to find out if they are dead or alive."

"General, may I volunteer the same task force we used to locate the two younger girls?" Baldwin asked.

General Miles chuckled. "You will be the vanguard, but I intend to use a force of sufficient strength to convince the Indians they will have no choice other than to surrender the girls if they have them, and then return to the reservation."

"General, how soon do you plan to get the expedition started?" one of the officers asked.

"Tomorrow morning at six," General Miles answered resolutely. "You're dismissed now to make such preparations as may be necessary."

All the officers came to attention and saluted, then turned to leave.

"Billy, Cade, if General Miles is giving everyone else until tomorrow, I want us to take to the field within an hour," Baldwin said.

BEFORE NIGHTFALL, Baldwin's scout had located a trail that although it looked to be no more than ten horses, seemed promising.

"This could be our first lead," Cade said. "A small group like this isn't going to stay out by themselves for very long."

"Not when they know every inch of the plains is crawlin' with soldiers, ready to shoot 'em anytime they see one of 'em," Billy said.

THE TROOPERS FOLLOWED the trail for several miles, until they came to some high bluffs that dropped down to a stream below. The troopers had come from a northeasterly direction, and overlooking the bluffs, they saw a horseshoe bend below them. Here the stream turned southwest, then nearly due south before settling back into its generally southwesterly direction.

Many lodges had been placed close to the stream, and as the soldiers approached them, they could see people running from the camp. Several were dashing up the bluffs that rose above the village, heading for a small herd of horses that was grazing there. An even larger number were headed downstream, where another horse herd was located.

"They're getting away!" one of the soldiers called.

"Let's go after them!" Henely ordered, leading his soldiers down the draw that led to the stream.

As they charged through the draw, Cade saw several armed Indians taking cover in holes, and others under the shelter of the sloping bank above the bench where the lodges were located. He knew then that this band of Indians planned to stay and fight rather than run.

When the soldiers reached the bottom of the draw, Cade had a closer and better look at the stream, and he realized that it was considerably deeper than he or anyone else had initially thought. However, there was no time to look for a more favorable crossing point, and when Cade rode into the stream, Baldwin, Henely, and two others followed him into the cold water. Their horses nearly foundered, but after a struggle, they made it across.

It was not until Henely gained the opposite side of the stream that he noticed the majority of the soldiers had not come with them. He saw a sergeant just on the other side.

"Sergeant Papier! Come on!" Henely shouted.

"Lieutenant, it's impossible to cross here!" Papier called back.

"We're here, Sergeant!" Henely called back. "How the hell do you think we got here if we didn't cross? You bring the troops across now, or I'll have your stripes!"

Taking a deep breath to steel himself, Papier called to the others, then plunged his horse into the water.

There was a lot of thrashing around, and several of the troopers were unhorsed, but by clinging to their saddles, they finally made it across. Not one man was lost during the effort, although one of the privates lost his carbine and another his pistol.

Once his men were across and reassembled, the troopers started after the Indians. More than half of them had made good their escape, but there were several who either hadn't had the opportunity to escape or had intentionally stayed to fight. These warriors positioned themselves along the crest of the nearby ridge.

The Indians began firing.

"Form a skirmish line!" Henely ordered.

Cade started to join the skirmish line, but Lieutenant Baldwin called to him.

"Cade, let the troopers do it. Scouts will stay back and cover the rear."

Cade nodded and took his position with the other scouts, watching as the soldiers advanced toward the Indians. Then, out of the corner of his eye, Cade saw an Indian rise from behind a large rock and take aim at the advancing troops. Cade had no idea who the warrior was targeting, but he didn't give him time to shoot. Cade aimed toward the Indian, using his pistol rather than his rifle because it was quicker. The warrior was at the extreme edge of pistol range, but Cade figured that even if he didn't hit him, a close miss would pull the shooter off target.

It was better than a close miss. Cade saw a little spray of blood erupt from the entry wound in the temple. The Indian dropped his rifle, unfired, and fell in place.

After the initial outbreak of shooting, wildly inaccurate on both sides, Lieutenant Henely ordered his men into the prone position. After that, the soldiers' firing became much more accurate, and attrition began to take its toll among the Indians. Then they saw a white flag fluttering as one of the Indians rose from his hiding place.

"Cease fire, cease fire!" Henely shouted, and the shooting stopped. Two Indians crawled up from their defensive positions and started toward the soldiers. One was a young warrior, the other was an old man. The old man was carrying the white flag.

"Sergeant Papier, do you recognize them?" Lieutenant Henely asked.

"I don't know the young one, sir, but the old one is called Dirty Water. He speaks English."

"All right, go parley with them."

"Yes, sir," Papier replied. Papier stood and, holding both hands up and clutching a white handkerchief in one hand, he started toward the two Indians. As the distance closed between them, Sergeant Papier called, "Dirty Water, my friend, why do we fight?"

"We fight no more," Dirty Water replied.

"That is good. It is time this war was end...uhnn!" He suddenly cried out in pain.

The cause of Papier's outcry was an Indian, who, lying in a depression, rose up and shot Sergeant Papier.

When the soldiers saw Sergeant Papier go down, all of them, without a specific order to do so, opened fire. The shooter, as well as Dirty Water and the young warrior who had come under the white flag, went down. After more shooting, the return fire from the Indians stopped, and Henely called for a cease-fire among his troops.

There was a long moment of silence until Henely called, "Any of you still alive, raise your hands and come out!"

There was no response to Henely's offer.

"Lieutenant, why don't Billy and I make our way in there and find out if anybody's left?" Cade asked Lieutenant Baldwin.

"Are you sure you want to do that?" Baldwin replied.

"We can't just stay here like this forever," Billy said. "Somebody's got to go in first."

"Austin," Baldwin called to Lieutenant Henely, "tell your men not to get trigger happy. McCall and Dixon are going in."

"All right, boys, go ahead," Henely called back.

Cade laid his rifle down and, pulling his pistol, headed toward the Indians' defensive position, with Billy covering him from about ten yards behind. Cade walked carefully, constantly sweeping his eyes from one end of the bluff to the other, being hyper-sensitive to the slightest movement. He stopped when he was about five yards short.

"Come on out," he called. "Come on out with your hands up."

Cade got no response to his offer. Cocking his pistol, he stepped all the way up to the depression.

He saw fourteen Indians, and all fourteen were dead.

GENERAL MILES WAS LOOKING AT A PICTURE OF TWO CHILDREN.

"Mrs. Miles sent this for you," Dr. Powers said. "It's the German girls."

The general looked more closely at the picture. Addie was sitting, and Julia was standing beside her with her hand on Addie's shoulder. Both girls were wearing cloaks and caps.

"I can't believe these are the same two little girls who left here such a short time ago," the General said. "I have to tell you, I wasn't sure they would survive the trip."

"Mrs. Miles was so kind to them, and they took to her right away."

"That's my Mary. How I wish we could get this campaign over so I could be with her," General Miles said.

"It has to be soon. When you see the Indians coming into the agencies, they are without horses or shelter or even food. Those who are still out are fools. They don't even have the ammunition to go after buffalo," Dr. Powers said.

"There was a Kiowa who rode into camp a few days ago. Will you send him in to see me?"

"Yes, sir."

. . .

Hawk Wing was not technically a scout, but he had provided information to the Army in the past, and General Miles had reason to trust him.

"You say you know where the two white girls are being held?"

Hawk Wing nodded. "The camp of Stone Calf."

"Four horses," Miles said, holding up his hand to display four fingers. "I will give you four horses if you will take this picture and put it into the hands of one of the white girls in Stone Calf's camp."

Hawk Wing shook his head. "Too dangerous."

"I know. That's why I'll give you four horses to do it."

"Four horses, one girl. Two girls, eight horses."

General Miles laughed. "What a bargainer you are, Hawk Wing. I'll give you eight horses."

"I pick?"

"Yes, you can pick, but you can't have my horse."

Hawk Wing grinned as he reached for the picture.

"Wait," Miles said. "I want to write a note to them."

He turned the picture over and began to write.

Jan. 21st, 1875. To the Misses Germain. These Germain sisters are well and are now with their friends. Do not be discouraged, efforts are being made for your benefit. Signed, Nelson A. Miles, Col. and Bvt. Maj. Gen. U.S. Army

The general was not aware he had misspelled the girls' name.

With the Cheyenne

Catherine and Sophia were brought before the council and ordered to sit while the council met.

"May I speak?" Catherine asked.

"You may speak," Stone Calf replied.

"I know that all here are wise men, and all here can speak the language of the whites. Since you are going to be talking about my sister and me, I ask that you speak in the language of our people so we may understand."

The members of the council held a spirited and sometimes angry discussion of Catherine's request. She was able to follow some but not all of the discussion until finally, Stone Calf spoke to her in English.

"We will talk in your tongue," he agreed.

Stone Calf turned to address the council.

"Never has it been so cold as it is now," Stone Calf said. "We try to run from the Long Knives, but each day, we can go only a little way. Our people are dying because of the cold. Our people are dying because we have little to eat. Our women cry in the lodges because they see their children die.

"I believe the Great Spirit Maheo has brought this upon us as punishment for keeping the two white girls. We must let them go, or the punishment will continue."

"The wagon was attacked, and many were killed," Medicine Water said. "We took four prisoners, and now we have only two. We must keep them. If we give them up, the Long Knives will punish us."

"Not all of our people did this evil thing," Stone Calf said. "I say we let them go."

"You let your captive go," Medicine Water said. "I not let mine go."

"Yes," Grey Beard said. "Stone Calf, we will let the old one go but we keep the young one. We make better bargain."

Stone Calf looked at Catherine. "You go," he said. He pointed to Sophia. "She stay."

"No!" Catherine said, putting her arms around Sophia. "I will not leave my sister."

"Catherine, you have to go," Sophia insisted.

"No! I won't leave you!"

The two girls clung together, staring defiantly at the council.

Stone Calf nodded. "You brave."

. . .

A COUPLE OF WEEKS LATER, a blanket-wrapped Indian approached Catherine. He wasn't anyone she had ever seen before but he didn't seem belligerent, so she felt no immediate fear.

"I am Hawk Wing," the Indian said. Reaching beneath his blanket, he pulled out a photograph and showed it to her.

"Oh!" she said. "Oh! Oh!" Tears of joy filled her eyes as she looked at the picture of her two little sisters. "They are alive! I must tell Sophia!"

Hawk Wing turned the picture over so Catherine could read General Miles' note on the back.

Do not be discouraged. Efforts are being made for your benefit.

When Catherine read those words, she began to tremble. Every night, she had prayed for some sign from God that this ordeal would end. Now, for the first time, she had hope that their captivity might indeed end.

When she could speak, she spoke to the man, clutching the picture to her breast.

"Thank you. I will show this picture to my sister."

"No!" Hawk Wing said. "I take it."

"Why? Sophia would want to see it, too."

"If Medicine Water know I come into his band, he kill me. I am Kiowa."

"Of course. You risked your life to bring it to me." Reluctantly, she handed the picture back to Hawk Wing. "Tell the white chief my sister and I will be waiting for him."

CATHERINE STEPPED outside the tipi and watched as the Kiowa made his way through the camp, then climbed the canyon wall and disappeared. Catherine hurried to Sophia's tent.

"SOPHIA, Julia and Addie are alive! They are well, and they are free!"

199

"How do you know this?"

"It's true. I saw their picture."

"Where did you see a picture?" Sophia demanded. "Let me see it too."

"I can't. A Kiowa snuck into this camp to show us the picture. On the back was a note from a general that said the Army is looking for us. They know we are alive, Sophia. Do you know what that means?"

"Oh, Catherine," Sophia said as tears began to stream down her face. "When? When will they come?"

"The Kiowa didn't say. We'll just have to be ready to escape when we hear the guns."

TWO DAYS LATER, Sophia came running into Catherine's tent in a state of near-panic. "Catherine, they want to kill me!"

"What happened?"

"I was scraping a deerskin for Quiet Fawn when Big Bow pointed his rifle at me and pulled the trigger! The cap popped, but the powder didn't explode. I ran away as fast as I could."

"Maybe there was no powder in the gun," Catherine suggested. "Maybe he was trying to scare you. We can't let anything happen to us now that we know the Army is coming to save us."

General Miles' Encampment

"GENERAL, Hawk Wing reported that Stone Calf's followers are desperate. They're out of ammunition, their horses are too weak, the warriors are weak, and their women and children are dying," Cade said.

"This is true," Miles replied. "We know where they are, we know they're too weak to fight us, and we know they're too weak to run away."

"But," Cade said, holding up his finger, "they are holding one weapon over us. If we attack, they'll kill the two girls."

"Unfortunately, this too is true."

"I have a suggestion if I may."

"I want those two girls released with every ounce of my being," General Miles said, "so I am open to any and all suggestions."

"I want to go to the village, and I want to take a man I know from one of the agencies with me. His name is Jesse Morrison, and he's the son-in-law of one of Grey Beard's chiefs. He tells me he can get me in safely."

"All right, suppose you can get into the village. What are your plans then?"

"I want to take in an ambulance. My plan is to bring the girls out."

Miles chuckled. "Don't you think that's a pretty ambitious plan?"

"Yes, sir, it is, but I believe the time has come to try it."

"All right," General Miles said. "The only thing I can say is you have my blessing."

IT HAD BEEN three days since General Miles had approved Cade's plan to enter Stone Calf's camp. Miles had insisted that at least six armed soldiers accompany him and Morrison. They camped the night before, quite literally within view of the Cheyenne camp, and the soldiers had arranged fallen logs and rocks to provide a defensive position should they need one.

"They didn't attack," Cade said as he finished a cup of coffee. "And you know they know we're here. I believe if we just go in, they won't do anything."

"I think you're right," Morrison said.

"Mr. McCall, if we hear shootin', we're comin' on in," Sergeant Carter said.

"No," Cade replied, holding up his hand. "If you hear shooting, it means I've misjudged the situation, and I want you and the others to get out of here as fast as you can."

It took only a few minutes to drive the ambulance from where they had bivouacked the night before to the Cheyenne village. As they came into the village, several Indians came out into the cold to watch their entry. They seemed to be a dispirited group of people, indeed.

When the ambulance stopped, the two men jumped down.

"Morrison," someone said. "Is that you?"

"Pévevóona'o," Morrison replied. "Good morning. We've come to talk to Stone Calf."

"I will take you to him," the man who had recognized Morrison said.

Stone Calf met them in the middle of the village and motioned for them to follow him into the council lodge. Grey Beard, Long Knife, and Medicine Water were in the council lodge.

"You have come for the white girls," Stone Calf said.

"Yes"

"What will you give us?" Grey Beard asked.

"We know your women are crying because their children are cold and do not have enough to eat. We know that every day, more of your people die from starvation and from sickness.

"The Great White Chief in Washington has given the agency at Darlington three hundred thousand dollars for food and blankets for all who live there. Many Cheyenne have already returned, and they are no longer hungry, they are not cold, and they celebrate their rituals without fear.

"This can all be yours," Cade said,

The chiefs were quiet for a moment.

"If you choose not to come in," Cade added, "think of this. You are weak, you have few guns left, and your horses cannot run. The Army has strong horses and men who are not hungry. We have many guns and many bullets. If you do not come in, we will destroy your village and kill many of your people."

"If you do that, we will kill the two white girls," Medicine Water said.

"That will not stop us," Cade said. "You will kill two of us, we will kill all of you."

ONE OF THE good things that had come from the recent council meeting was that Catherine and Sophia were now allowed to stay in the same lodge. They were just finishing their breakfast of cooked mule meat when Stone Calf came in. A moment later, two white men stepped into the lodge.

"Mr. McCall!" Catherine said, recognizing the man who had been her father's friend. "What? What are you doing here?"

"I have come to take you and your sister away from here," Cade told her.

With little cries of joy, both Catherine and Sophia moved to Cade and embraced him, crying happily as they did so. Then, seeing Jesse Morrison, and knowing only that he was a white man, they embraced him as well.

"Little Squaw is happy for you but sad to see you go." Looking toward the lodge opening, Catherine saw Little Squaw standing there with tears streaming down her face.

"Little Squaw, you are my friend, and I will never forget you," Catherine said as she moved toward the woman to embrace her.

WHEN THE AMBULANCE rolled down the road to the Darlington Cheyenne agency early in the evening of the next day, both sides of the road were lined for half a mile with white soldiers, black soldiers, officers and their wives, friendly Cheyenne and Arapaho, and other Darlington personnel. They waved hats and hands, and they shouted happy welcomes to the two girls who were riding on the front seat behind the driver. Cade was riding alongside the girls. "Mr. McCall, do you believe in Heaven?" Catherine asked.

"Yes, I do," Cade said, surprised by the question.

"Then you know that Papa and Mama, Stephen and Rebecca and

Joanna are all there looking down, and they're heaping their blessings on you for what you've done for us."

"And I feel that blessing," Cade replied. "But my biggest blessing has been getting to know you and your sisters. You will remember what you have just been through forever, Catherine, and while they will be bad memories, you can also take pride in the courage and strength that you, all four of you, showed. That strength and courage will serve you for the rest of your lives.

EPILOGUE

Twin Creek Ranch, Howard County, Texas—1927

OWEN WISTER WIPED HIS EYES, THEN FOLDED UP THE HANDKERCHIEF and stuck it in his pocket.

"Excuse me," he said. "I apologize for that, I'm not generally so emotional, but that..."

"There's no need to apologize, Dan," Cade said. "There was not a dry eye among any of the soldiers when we found Julia and Addie, nor among those who were lining Darlington Road the day Catherine and Sophia were freed."

"What became of the girls?

"A couple named Patrick and Louisa Corney became Julia and Addie's legal guardians, and the girls lived with them until they graduated from high school. Then Catherine married Louisa's brother; Amos Swerdfeger was his name. After they got married, the whole bunch, including the German girls, moved to Nemaha County, Nebraska and went to farming some good land. I think the government gave each of the girls a twenty-five-hundred-dollar settlement when everything was over. I believe the last girl got married about 1893, and I think they all had children of their own."

"General Miles, Colonel Mackenzie, and Lieutenant Baldwin certainly played a big role in this saga," Wister said. "But they wound up playing a significant role in American history."

"They did indeed," Cade said. "Unfortunately, Makenzie died before he could fulfill his destiny, but Miles went on to reach the highest rank possible, Commanding General of the Army. And this from a man who had not attended West Point.

"Before we started on this tale, you pointed out my Medal of Honor, which, as I explained, was rescinded. Now, Frank Baldwin—he was the genuine hero. Received two Medals of Honor, and went on to serve as a general in the World War. Frank Baldwin and I became good friends over the years, and we maintained contact until he died in 1923."

"Cade, have you ever thought about how much history you've influenced?" Owen asked.

Cade chuckled. "That comes with living to a ripe old age."

"No, it comes from being a man who has an indomitable will, a great amount of courage, a code of honor, and a strong sense of right and wrong. Only when those ingredients meet opportunity can a man help shape national events. You are just such a man." Owen smiled. "That's why I am writing the *Adventures of Cade McCall*. I can't wait to find out where we are going next."

A LOOK AT THE GOLD TRAIN: A FARADAY NOVEL

BY ROBERT VAUGHAN

INTRODUCING MATTHEW FARADAY...

The train-top murder of one of his female operatives has thrust Matthew Faraday, the wily chief of Faraday Security Service, into the dark and twisting tunnel of another railroad mystery, and a coded message in the dead woman's pocket is the only clue.

Don't miss this novel in the Faraday western by bestselling author Robert Vaughan.

AVAILABLE NOW ON AMAZON

ABOUT THE AUTHOR

Robert Vaughan sold his first book when he was 19. That was 57 years and nearly 500 books ago. He wrote the novelization for the miniseries *Andersonville*. Vaughan wrote, produced, and appeared in the History Channel documentary *Vietnam Homecoming*. His books have hit the NYT bestseller list seven times. He has won the Spur Award, the PORGIE Award (Best Paperback Original), the Western Fictioneers Lifetime Achievement Award, received the Readwest President's Award for Excellence in Western Fiction, is a member of the American Writers Hall of Fame and is a Pulitzer Prize nominee. Vaughn is also a retired army officer, helicopter pilot with three tours in Vietnam. And received the Distinguished Flying Cross, the Purple Heart, The Bronze Star with three oak leaf clusters, the Air Medal for valor with 35 oak leaf clusters, the Army Commendation Medal, the Meritorious Service Medal, and the Vietnamese Cross of Gallantry.